PREY ZONE

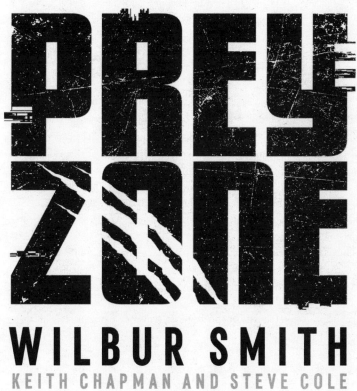

WILBUR SMITH

KEITH CHAPMAN AND STEVE COLE

HOT
KEY
BOOKS

First published in Great Britain in 2022 by
HOT KEY BOOKS
4th Floor, Victoria House, Bloomsbury Square
London WC1B 4DA
Owned by Bonnier Books
Sveavägen 56, Stockholm, Sweden
www.hotkeybooks.com

A CIP catalogue record for this book is available from the British Library.

ISBN: 978-1-4714-1245-5
Also available as an ebook and in audio

1

This book is typeset using Atomik ePublisher
Printed and bound in Great Britain by Clays Ltd, Elcograf S.p.A.

Hot Key Books is an imprint of Bonnier Books UK
www.bonnierbooks.co.uk

This book is dedicated to all uprising scouts who will proudly carry on our work – to keep protecting all life on Mother Earth.

Wilbur Smith

N

PRETORIA

High security perimeter fence

JOSEF GERHARD GAME RESERVE

Predasaur pens

Gerhard's complex

Comms blackout zone

DOWNRIVER

Restricted area

Entrance to VIP compound

Ravine

Elephant

Boulder Point

Recovery Pens

HUNTING LODGES

HUNTING LODGES

LEBOMBO MOUNTAINS

MAIN ROAD

CROCODILE LODGE GAME RESERVE

MAIN HOUSE

TOURIST LODGES

CROCODILE RIVER

GAUDA

UPRIVER

MAP NOT DRAWN TO SCALE

PROLOGUE

The place: Josef Gerhard Game Reserve, South Africa

Time: The near future

Panting, Dane Mellanby leaned hard against the trunk of a jackalberry tree. The stitch in his side felt like hot knives in his ribs, and sweat stung his eyes. He'd been running like hell through the thorny undergrowth. His hands were more bloody scratches than skin, but he felt no pain. Only terror, and sheer desperation to escape.

Mellanby pulled at the high neck of the jumpsuit he'd been forced to wear. It was dotted with reflective markers that dazzled ruby-red in the midday sunlight – and the damn thing couldn't be removed. It was choking him.

A thin mechanical buzz knifed through the heavy stillness. Mellanby saw a silver sphere with a dark eye – a camera drone – bob into sight through the trees.

So . . . they *were* watching him. Recording every fearful, sweat-soaked moment.

And Mellanby knew the sickening reason why.

Keeping his head down, he ignored the drone and pushed onwards. Behind him, he could hear the hungry howl of the *thing* that was chasing him. It was so much closer now. Mellanby knew he couldn't keep running much longer. His sides were burning, breath scraping at his throat. Finally, he staggered and fell to his knees. Two drones buzzed about him like steel hornets. Ahead of him was a thicket of mopane and red bushwillow trees.

Climb, he thought. *Get out of the thing's reach.*

Then, beyond the trees, he glimpsed a chain-link fence rising from the grassland, perhaps ten metres high. The perimeter fence. Another drone hovered close by.

If he could only scale it and reach the other side, he might stand a chance of escaping.

He heard something heavy crash through the thicket behind him, then the whine of an electric engine. It was a vehicle. Could it be coming to his rescue? It sounded as if it was approaching fast.

But the beast was approaching faster. Mellanby heard its deep growl, the thud of its heavy paws in the long grass.

He forced himself up and ran for the fence as if the devil was behind him.

In reality, it was something worse.

The beast pounded over the dusty ground and gave a shriek of triumph. Mellanby saw its red eyes narrow, its huge jaws crank open.

He knew he had seconds to live.

Desperate, he jumped for the chain-link fence and began to climb. A moment later the beast slammed against the fence, which shook like a sail in the wind. Mellanby was almost thrown free. A drone dropped down to his head height, scanning him. Mellanby closed his eyes and whimpered, not daring to look down as he climbed higher. The colossal beast jumped up, clawing at the fence. Moaning with fear, Mellanby clung on, sweat-soaked and shaking.

The blare of a horn, like the call of a cavalry, stirred the dusty air. Mellanby turned, blinked tears from his eyes, and saw a luxury model jeep skid to a stop maybe eighty metres away. The beast turned to face this new arrival with a roar of defiance.

Thank God, thought Mellanby. *Gerhard's come to his senses. He only wanted to scare me into keeping quiet, not kill me.*

The man in the passenger seat stepped carefully down from the jeep and signalled to the men inside. 'No one shoot. Not yet.'

Mellanby saw who it was. 'You . . . ?' For a moment, his grip on reality slackened. His grip on the fence slackened too.

The beast, as if sensing that Mellanby was off-guard, reared up and slammed its powerful forepaws against the fence. Mellanby screamed as he lost his hold on the fence and fell six metres. His right ankle buckled as he hit the ground. The pain was so intense that he thought he would pass out.

He didn't.

He was still conscious as the beast closed its jaws around his injured ankle and tore at it in a vicious frenzy. Mellanby would have screamed again, but a giant paw was pressing down on his throat, crushing, suffocating. He thrashed in the crimson grass as if drowning as the mantrap jaws bit down.

Two men with automatic weapons stepped down from the jeep, keeping the beast covered while it tore Mellanby apart. Their leader joined them, calmly watching the beast as it fed.

'It's only fair that the condemned should enjoy a last meal, eh?' he said. Kneeling, he took careful aim with his bolt-action rifle. From this distance, a Bell shot – angling the bullet through the neck and into the brain for an instant kill – was a huge challenge. But if he only wounded the beast it might bolt away to die in the bush, where its body would be lost to a dozen scavengers. He wasn't losing a trophy like this.

The shot was perfect. The powerful beast jerked . . . and died.

The hunter accepted the applause of his companions and posed for photographs as Mellanby's blood soaked slowly into fur, skin and soil.

The hunter was smiling.

1

The grass in the bushveld was dry and dusty. Shield bugs and flower beetles glinted as they buzzed lazily through the heat, their shells shimmering shades of blue and green in the sunlight. Ralph and Robyn Ballantyne took a rest beside the enormous barrel-like trunk of the largest baobab tree in their father's game reserve. This one was almost twenty metres tall; they used it as a landmark on many of their adventures. Its beautiful white flowers had faded weeks ago with the end of spring, and January's summer heat wrapped around them both.

Ralph took advantage of the shade the baobab's spreading, many-fingered branches provided, and sipped from his water bottle. He watched his sister as she crouched beside an elephant's footprint. They had risen at six a.m. and spent two hours following the huge bull's tracks, which made smooth impressions like large dinner plates.

'How far ahead do you think he is, Rob?' Ralph asked.

'Can't be far.' Robyn, fifteen and one year Ralph's senior, smoothed her long dark hair back from her eyes. 'The grass is still bending back here from where he's stepped on it. Here, boost me up to that branch, will you?'

Launching from the stirrup of Ralph's hands, Robyn scaled the tree with an easy grace and pulled out her field binoculars. She peered around, scanning the veldt for any trace of the elephant. If he'd forced his way through the forest he would have left clear signs behind. If not, he must have detoured around the forest, towards the stream that fed into the river.

'Just think,' Ralph said. 'If you didn't enjoy sorting through giant mounds of elephant crap we could be swimming right now.'

Robyn glanced down at him from her vantage point in the tree. 'And an elephant could be starving to death,' she said pointedly.

The day before, while trekking down to the river that ran alongside the reserve, she had found a knee-high pile of muck containing whole leaves and twigs.

'It must've come from an old elephant,' she'd told their dad at dinner last night. 'His teeth must be really worn down because he can't chew his food properly. He needs our help.'

'What are we supposed to do, cut up his grub for him?' Ralph had joked.

'We can make certain that he's not in pain,' Robyn argued. 'That he has a decent quality of life.'

'Well said,' Dad agreed.

Roland Ballantyne's love for Africa and its animals had deep roots stretching back through generations of his family, and he'd passed that love on to his children. In wilder days, Roland's grandfather had stocked his ranches with prime cattle; now, Roland was the guardian of a rich ecosystem that he worked hard to maintain. In the Crocodile Lodge Game Reserve, protecting endangered species, keeping track of animal numbers, and ensuring a healthy balance of prey and predators formed part of everyone's responsibilities.

Ralph squinted up at his sister as she scanned the veldt. He sighed. 'I wish Dad would let us do something a bit more exciting than trailing old elephants.'

Robyn snorted. 'You know what he's like. "Since your mum died, you're all I've got. I can't lose you too, blah blah blah . . ."'

Ralph winced and nodded. Seven years ago, the whole family had caught the Ebola virus. Some quirk of Roland's immune system had saved him, a genetic lifeline that by fluke he'd passed on to his children and which helped their bodies fight off the virus and recover. But their mum had no such protection, and she was one of the ones who died.

'I get that he doesn't want anything to happen to us,' said Ralph. 'But that means nothing *ever* happens.' He tapped his fingers against the Smith & Wesson Mercox dart gun he carried in his hip holster. 'We'll spend our whole lives plodding about like this old elephant.'

'*You're* all right,' Robyn said. 'It's me that Dad's sending on work experience with his girlfriend tomorrow. As if I want to be a nurse – like she is.'

'You totally know she's not a nurse; she's a professor,' Ralph pointed out. 'Anyway, it's school that's sending you. Dad's just keeping it in the family.'

'Niko is not family,' Robyn snapped, then saw the wicked grin on Ralph's face. She scowled, hating how easily he could wind her up. 'Anyway, it's a waste of time. I'm going to work with animals when I'm older. Not people.'

'Until Niko opens your eyes to the wonders of human medicine,' said Ralph cheerily.

'Oh, go smooch a yawning leopard!' Robyn put the binoculars back to her eyes. 'There's no sign of the elephant. He must have gone to drink or bathe in the river. If he walked on through the water, there'll be no tracks.' She was about to lower the binoculars again when a flash of contrast caught her eye. A strip of something dark hung from a broken branch near the riverbank at the edge of the forest. And it looked like blood had been spilled on the ground.

Robyn dropped lithely from the baobab tree to the ground. 'Wait here,' she said. 'I just want to check something.'

'Knock yourself out,' said Ralph. 'Not literally. I don't want to carry you back.'

'Like you even could,' Robyn retorted.

Ralph watched her stride away through the long grass towards the forest edge. He felt a twinge of guilt for teasing her. It soon faded, though. He didn't like the way Robyn treated Niko; she was a good, caring person, and he was glad Dad had grown close to someone since losing Mum. Robyn wasn't so happy about it, even though Mum and Niko had been friends. The two of them had even worked together during the Ebola outbreak that took their mum's life.

That was the problem, Ralph supposed: Mum had died

and Niko hadn't. And as far as Robyn was concerned, Niko was stepping into Mum's old life. Ralph was sure that was why their dad was pushing Robyn into work experience with Niko. First, it would help Robyn to see Niko as a caring health worker, not a scheming man-stealer. Second, spending time with people instead of animals, for once, might just make Rob understand them a bit better.

Ralph's brooding was interrupted by a rustling, and a crunching that came from the undergrowth in the direction of the river. A large animal was on the move: the elephant, maybe. He turned towards Robyn. She was studying the ground by the trees, as if looking for tracks. Ralph shrugged. If she could go off by herself, so could he.

Quietly, he ducked into the undergrowth, swinging himself nimbly through leafy bushes and gnarled branches, following the sounds.

Then he heard it.

Ralph had lived alongside the animals of the bush all his life. He knew the sounds of prey running for their lives and the howls of triumphant predators. But this sound was like nothing he had ever heard: a deep, wheezing rasp, and the clack and grind of powerful jaws. A desperate yowling roar sounded beneath it, made by something else – a big cat, maybe?

What the hell was going on?

Ralph's first instinct was to run. But on the other hand, hadn't he just been craving excitement? And if an animal was hurt and needed help . . .

He pulled the dart gun from his holster and quickened

his step. With his left hand, he grabbed his satellite phone from his back pocket to call Robyn – just as it buzzed in his hand to say that she was calling *him*.

'Rob,' he said breathlessly, still pushing through the undergrowth. 'Listen.'

'No, you listen!' Robyn said urgently. 'I've found something here.'

'I've *heard* something!' he shot back. 'I don't know what it is, but . . .'

The words died in his throat as a shaggy, sand-coloured blur of muscle bounded past, almost knocking him over. He dropped the phone in shock and stood as still as stone.

I was nearly run down by a lion, he thought numbly. *It didn't even notice me. Chasing down prey? Or running for its life . . . ?*

Next moment, the snap of branches and the pounding of heavy feet signalled new danger. Something else was beating a path through the vegetation. Through swaying boughs, Ralph glimpsed a massive dark shape rush after the lion with horrifying speed. The ground seemed to shake as it passed – or was that just the hammering of Ralph's heart?

As suddenly as it had arrived, the thing was gone.

'It can't have been chasing the lion,' Ralph breathed. 'Lions have no predators apart from humans . . .'

Hunters could take many forms, but the dark shape he'd glimpsed? It looked somehow wrong. Unearthly.

'Ralph!' Robyn's voice broke tinnily from the phone. 'Will you stop playing around and get back here?'

'Damn right I will.' Ralph scooped up the phone, ended the call and ran back the way he'd come. He gripped the dart gun as he ran, his knuckles white, as if it was a charm that could ward off nameless horrors.

2

Robyn was waiting for Ralph at the forest's edge. As he ran into sight, she frowned. He was pale and sweaty.

'You look like you've seen a ghost,' she said. 'What happened?'

Ralph hesitated. 'I saw a lion being chased, I think,' he said eventually. 'No idea what was after it. I didn't see it clearly.'

'Something with a death wish, presumably.'

'But it was massive, and so fast. I . . . I don't know what it was.' Ralph blew out a shaky breath. 'I guess it had the lion's scent so strongly in its nostrils, it didn't notice me.'

'There's no meat on you anyway,' she teased, trying to joke him out of it. But Ralph still looked haunted. Robyn felt a stab of concern. 'This lion you saw – it wasn't Jari or Sabal, was it?'

'I couldn't tell,' Ralph admitted.

Robyn looked downcast. She had helped to rear Jari and Sabal when their mother was killed by hunters. They had formed a deep bond that persisted to this day, even now the cubs were full-grown adults.

Time to change the subject, Ralph thought and wiped his clammy hands on his top. 'What were you calling for, anyway? What did you find?'

'This.' Robyn held up a length of tough grey material. 'Hanging from a low tree branch at the forest's edge. What do you make of it?'

'It's some sort of heavy-duty strap,' said Ralph. He fingered the frayed end. 'Something's cut through it.'

'I think it was attached to a harness worn by an animal,' Robyn said. She pointed at the mud between them and the river. 'Look at these tracks.'

The little heart-shaped tracks in the bloodstained mud were clear and unmistakable.

'Springbok,' Ralph said. As a child, he had loved the little antelope above all other animals: it was South Africa's national animal, and its hoof prints had been the first he'd learned to recognise.

'No sign of the predator,' noted Robyn, trying to make sense of the story told by the soil. 'But look how the rear hoof prints overstep the front.'

'It was running. Running fast,' Ralph said. 'Like the lion.'

Robyn looked at him. 'You think this is linked to what you saw?'

'No clue,' said Ralph. 'But it's obvious that the springbok was attacked by something – something that cut through the strap of the harness it wore.'

'It managed to get away, though,' Robyn said. 'There'd be more blood if it had been killed here, and a clear trail if the body had been dragged off by predators.' Robyn tucked the strap into her belt. 'I guess the elephant will have to wait. The springbok's definitely injured, and from the size of the tracks it must be young.'

'It needs help,' Ralph agreed. 'We have to find it. We can keep an eye out for any signs of the lion too.'

'And whatever was chasing it,' Robyn added gravely. 'Anything that can make a lion run like that is something we need to learn more about.'

She led the way carefully through the bushland, tracking the injured springbok. She and Ralph fell into an easy coordinated pace side by side, as they had done for years. Now that he knew what he was looking for, Ralph pointed out details as they tracked – tiny drops of blood, broken blades of grass, half-prints in the terrain.

It took them twenty minutes to find the little antelope, a ewe, with no sign of the lion or its pursuer. Ralph was beginning to think he'd imagined the whole thing. The springbok was real enough, though. She lay shaking under a red bushwillow tree, where she had tried to hide herself among the leaves and clusters of fruit. She lifted her head as the Ballantynes approached. From the set of the ewe's muscles and the tiny tremors in her movements, Robyn could tell the animal was in terrible pain. On closer inspection she saw the ewe's left hind leg was scored with a deep gash.

'Hello, girl,' Robyn whispered. Slowly, on all fours, she edged forward and stretched out a hand towards the ewe, breathing slowly. After a few moments the springbok lowered her head again and closed her eyes. Her shivering slowed. Robyn cleared away the leaves that covered her.

'I'll never know how you do that,' Ralph murmured. 'You're like a witch.'

'A witch who's spent most of her life with animals, studying their communication techniques,' said Robyn casually. She knew that was only part of it, though. She had always been able to connect with animals, to soothe them and make them trust her. Robyn could never explain how, but deep down she felt it stemmed from her connection to the land here; land that her family had loved and lived on for generations.

'The poor thing's wearing some sort of collar.' She fingered the tough material around the springbok's neck, fixed with a heavy Velcro fastener. The stub of a strap dangled from it.

'Matches the material you found on that branch,' Ralph noted. 'You were right – it was part of a lead. Somehow it pulled free.'

'Why would anyone try to take one of our springbok?' said Robyn. 'They're worth nothing to poachers. And a hunter would just shoot her, not take her for a walk.'

'That gash on her leg could have been made by a knife.'

'Or claws, maybe?' Robyn felt something of the springbok's own fear and confusion. From her trouser pocket she took a small packet and tore it open to reveal a folded piece of white gauze with blue threads running through it. 'The blue stuff's a clotting agent,' she explained to her brother. 'Helps prevent blood loss.'

Gently and carefully, Robyn bound the springbok's wounded leg. The animal didn't react, just lay in the grass, her breathing fast and shallow. 'She's in shock. We need to get her back to the Lodge for treatment.'

'It's time we were getting ready for class, anyway.' Ralph pulled out his phone. 'I'll get one of the rangers here with a pickup. A couple of nights in the recovery pens and our patient will be good as new.'

Robyn stared into the ewe's dark, fearful eyes. 'I hope so,' she murmured, and wondered just what the springbok – and Ralph – had seen.

That evening, when the sun was still warm, Ralph and Robyn paid a visit to the recovery pens. You could smell the place clear across the Lodge compound – a pungent cocktail of animals, dung and disinfectant.

For Ralph, the stink was like a vitamin shot in the arm after the sterile drudge of online school. The Lodge was too remote for them to take classes in person, so lessons over the internet were a necessary evil – and better than boarding, at least. And if they were needed for Lodge business, they could skip some classes, so long as they made up the time later.

Ralph had found it hard to concentrate today. The shadowy shape he'd seen in the forest haunted him. And of course, like Robyn, he was keen to know how the little springbok was getting on.

As they walked into the cooler shadows of the pens, Ralph saw his dad and smiled. His dad was looking down at the injured animal beside his friend and business partner, Xai. They were both in their usual working clothes – short-sleeved olive-green shirts and tan shorts. Roland

Ballantyne was tall and lean, his skin weathered bronze from a life spent outdoors, while Xai had the typical short stature of his tribe and dark skin that wrinkled early in life. A traditional hide bag was slung over one shoulder. Xai had worked extensively with Roland's Special Forces squadron, 'Ballantyne's Brigade', back in their combat days. They had saved each other's lives often enough to create a lifelong bond of friendship, and their work together had continued ever since. When Roland left the army to look after the Crocodile Lodge Game Reserve, Xai came with him and had lived in one of the staff cottages ever since. Xai had been part of Ralph and Robyn's lives since their birth. He had been a bedrock of stability for them all when their mother died.

The springbok was sleeping. Ralph noted that no fresh blood was showing through Robyn's bandage.

'Hey, kids,' said Roland. 'Well done – you saved this little one's life. If you hadn't found her and stopped the bleeding . . .'

'Thank goodness,' said Robyn. 'The wound isn't infected, is it?'

'I've cleaned it up,' Xai said. 'She'll be running about again in a couple of days.'

'It's who else might be running about here that troubles me,' said Roland.

Ralph raised an eyebrow. 'Meaning?'

'One of our rangers spotted intruders in the park today,' Xai told them.

'Poachers?' Robyn said the word like it stank; to her

there was nothing filthier than people who killed animals to make a profit.

'Poachers don't usually carry automatic weapons,' said Roland. 'And they aren't seen going downriver in military-grade amphibious craft.'

'Seriously?' Ralph stared at him. 'Downriver towards Gerhard's lodge?'

'To trespass there too?' Xai mused.

'Or to report back to their boss.' Roland sneered.

'You think Gerhard sent them?' Xai looked unconvinced. 'Why would he be fool enough to risk sending an armed patrol into our territory?'

'More intimidation tactics,' Roland suggested. 'He's been quiet lately. Probably preparing.'

Robyn's brow creased. 'Do you think he's lobbying to bring back trophy hunting again?'

Ralph sighed. Josef Gerhard was a billionaire tech giant and hunting enthusiast from the USA who had controversially been granted the right to buy half the Kruger National Park from the South African government two years ago – land adjacent to Crocodile Lodge and just across the river. He'd promised to revitalise animal numbers and boost the tourism industry. Unfortunately, his plan to do that involved bringing back trophy hunting – the practice of killing the biggest, most impressive wild animals purely for pleasure and bragging rights.

While supporters of trophy hunting touted it as a way to protect animals, claiming that hunters' fees for slaughtering the biggest game were ploughed back into conservation efforts, the Ballantynes stood squarely on the opposite side of the debate. Roland argued that trophy hunts killed animals with the rarest traits – prime specimens with the darkest manes or the largest tusks – and so led to a weaker, more vulnerable wild population. And he had played a key role in finally getting the practice banned some years back. Unwilling to let that good work go to hell on the whim of a greedy businessman who wasn't even a local, he'd led public protests, petitions and legal challenges against Gerhard's efforts to revive trophy hunting, and had blocked all Gerhard's attempts to overturn the law. Of course, in the process, he had made a powerful enemy who lived on his doorstep.

Ralph was just glad his dad didn't scare easily. Roland, with Xai at his side, had only become more determined in the face of the threats and harassment from Gerhard's staff. But it had made Roland's already protective attitude towards his kids that much fiercer.

'The first thing I'm going to do is get Van Rok and his team in to upgrade our comms network and surveillance systems,' Roland said firmly.

Ralph nodded. VanRok Security was an up-and-coming company run by Mr Van Rok, a regular visitor to Crocodile Lodge with his son Luke. 'Are you going to give in to technology and finally get some drones?' Ralph asked hopefully. 'I've been saying for ages you need camera drones here to properly keep an eye on the animals . . .'

Xai snorted softly; Ralph knew that he considered technological trackers little more than a toy, a pale imitation of the real thing. But Roland waved away his friend's concerns. 'Yes, drones, infrared sensors, more hidden cams, the works – as a priority. And at first light tomorrow, we're going out searching for any evidence these intruders have left behind.'

'Good,' said Robyn. 'I'll come with you.'

'You can't,' said Ralph. 'You're on call with our dear Dr Niko Haart from SangoMed Healthcare . . .'

'Work experience!' Robyn groaned. 'Dad, get me out of it. This is way more important!'

'No, Robyn. It's all been arranged. Niko's making a field visit tomorrow and she says she could really use your help.'

'Can I join you, Dad?' Ralph asked. 'I could show you where I saw the . . . whatever it was.'

Roland frowned. 'What?'

'Out on the trail I saw a lion being chased by something. I thought it was an animal of some kind – but what could be hounding a lion? Maybe it was the intruders.'

'Is this a joke?' Xai said warily.

'No, it's true,' Ralph insisted. 'It shot past me so fast, I didn't get a proper look at it. I can show you. First light tomorrow. I'd stay with you and Xai and not get in the way.'

'We'll see,' said Roland. Xai winked.

'So unfair,' Robyn muttered. She pushed past Roland and unbolted the springbok pen so she could take a closer look. 'Well,' she said, moving slowly inside. 'At least her eyes are brighter . . .' She stroked the springbok's head and neck, and the animal nuzzled closer to her. 'Wait a minute.' She was feeling the springbok's neck more closely

20

now. 'There's something under the skin. Something hard, like an implant.'

'Let me feel.' Xai joined her inside and felt around the springbok's fur with sure hands. 'Funny. Feels like a data tag.'

Ralph frowned. 'You don't chip the springbok, do you?'

'No, only the bigger animals,' Robyn said.

'I've got the tag-reader app.' Xai took out his satellite phone – which was identical to Ralph and Robyn's phones, as were all the handsets – and pressed it to the springbok's hide. 'If that really is a chip . . .'

There was a chime. Xai stared down at the screen, stony-faced. Then he showed it to Roland.

'This springbok belongs to the Josef Gerhard Reserve,' said Roland, with a snort. 'I bet he catalogues every last animal on his land, right down to the mosquitoes. All tech, no sense.'

'But how did one of Gerhard's springbok wind up on our land? And would that explain the armed intruders?' Ralph shook his head. 'Why would they take an amphibious landing craft downriver to recapture one little ewe?'

'She was wearing a harness,' Robyn reminded him. 'Someone didn't want her to run. Perhaps there's something special about her?'

'Xai, make sure she's monitored, will you?' said Roland. Xai nodded.

'Tomorrow we'll have a proper search around where the intruders were spotted.'

'Yes,' said Ralph. '*We* will. Some of us, anyway . . .'

Robyn scowled at him. Ralph gave her his most saintly

smile, contemplating the day ahead with a thrill of anticipation. He felt sorry for his sister, missing out, but she wouldn't want his sympathy. She was far too independent for that.

Neither of them knew it, but the next day would change both their lives for ever.

3

Robyn eyed the grassy banks through her shades as the speedboat raced upriver. She was perched on a bench seat, trailing her fingers through the dark water. Niko had the helm. Fit and sporty in her Goodyear baseball cap and navy-blue jumpsuit, she looked more like one of the Grand Prix pit crew out of Kyalami than a doctor. Though she would never admit to it, Robyn approved of Niko's unconventional streak.

The boat's electric engine was almost silent, but the wind and the water rushing past the shiny solar panels on the bows drowned out the chirrup of crickets and the call and croak of wading birds.

'Glad to have you along today, Robyn,' Niko said for the third time that morning.

Also for the third time that morning, Robyn answered with a noncommittal, 'Mmm.' As conversations between the two of them went, it was fairly typical.

'I'm actually pleased this field visit came up at the last minute,' Niko went on. 'I know you hate the idea of working in an office.'

23

'So what's actually happened?'

'Some people have gotten sick in a village called Gauda. I've been asked in by a colleague to give a second opinion.'

'What's the first opinion?' asked Robyn.

Niko paused. 'They don't know.'

Now Robyn stared at her. 'How can they not know? What if it's something dangerous?' Robyn shivered at the memory of her mother's death. 'I mean, Ebola-level serious.'

'Please don't worry, Robyn,' said Niko. 'The hospital team has isolated the patients and I'll be wearing full PPE when I examine them.'

'Personal protective equipment?'

'Exactly. There's no danger, and I'll set you up in the admin block. I'd love you to proofread a report I've written on zoonotic diseases for *Nature* magazine while I'm working, but if you'd rather . . . Well, if you want to just surf the web or something, that's fine too.'

Surf the web, thought Robyn with an inward groan. *How old are you, ninety?* But out loud, she said, 'Thanks,' with a touch more sarcasm than intended.

They both retreated into an awkward silence. It was a relief when they reached Gauda a long ten minutes later. Niko pulled back on the throttle, jostling the other boats aside to dock at the village's jetty.

There was no one to meet them. There was no one around at all.

'Bad sign,' Niko muttered as she climbed out of the boat. 'Looks like no one can be spared to drive us. Still, it's not so far.'

Niko hurried along the dirt road to the village, Robyn walking beside her. The morning was already warm, with a deep blue sky that stretched into infinity behind a few scattered white clouds. The sunny call of the orioles filled the air with music, but as they neared the village, the hum and buzz of the old generator drowned out the sounds of the natural world.

The village itself was a mixture of European-style cottages and modern versions of traditional African circular houses with thatched cones for roofs.

'Let's find the admin block,' Niko said, steering Robyn down a paved path. 'Oh, I see it. That's such an ugly glass building, doesn't fit in at all . . .' She trailed off as they rounded a corner and saw a medical team in hazard suits, loading a gurney into an ambulance. There was something large, white and glossy on the gurney.

A chill ran over her body, despite the heat of the morning, as Robyn realised it was a body bag. 'Someone's died?' she said. 'What of?'

Before Niko could answer, one of the medical workers saw her and hurried over. 'What the hell?' the young man cried. He looked exhausted. 'Why aren't you two wearing PPE? What are you doing here?'

'Dr Sabaya sent for me,' Niko explained. 'I'm Dr Niko Haart, professor of epidemiology and zoonotic diseases –'

'Oh, it's you. Thank God you're here, we weren't expecting you so soon.' The young man looked at Robyn. 'And you . . . ?'

'Uh . . .' Robyn, to her embarrassment, found herself tongue-tied. 'I'm just –'

'Robyn is my student assistant today,' Niko said, with a look her way that added silently, *OK?*

Robyn nodded curtly, not wanting to show her discomfort. 'You look like you've been up all night, Mr . . . ?'

'Dr Kiizu Ndlovu. Yes, I don't think anyone's slept. It's been kind of intense, you know?' He waved his gloved hand. 'We're treating this village as a contaminated area, so you'll both have to suit up. We have about twenty Patients Under Investigation in quarantine waiting to be assessed, and ten people with early symptoms being treated in the village hall.'

'As many as that?' said Niko softly. 'What's the progression of symptoms?'

'They start dry, with fever, joint aches, fatigue . . .'

'And wet symptoms?'

'Vomiting. Bleeding in the lungs. Uncontrollable coughing.'

Robyn felt her skin crawl. 'Sounds a bit like Ebola.'

'There are some similarities, but this seems to be an airborne infection while Ebola is spread through contact with blood or body flui—'

'I know!' Robyn snapped. She kept imagining her mum lying inside a body bag like the one on the gurney.

Niko stepped in smoothly. 'Who's looking at your patients, Dr Ndlovu?'

'We're a team of six, counting myself,' Kiizu said. 'And now we have you two. Come on, let's suit you up and take you to Dr Sabaya.' He gestured for Robyn and Niko to move ahead of him towards a large tent pitched on brown grass. 'Everything's through there in the donning area. I'll join you shortly.'

As Kiizu returned to the ambulance, Robyn followed Niko through a sealed plastic partition into the tent and found hand sanitiser and piles of protective equipment laid out on a table.

'Once more into the breach,' said Niko. 'Robyn, there's no call for you to join me at the frontline. Why don't you make your way to the admin block? I'm sure the staff there will –'

'This is work experience,' said Robyn, picking up a cloth gown she guessed was worn under the proper suit. 'I'm your assistant, aren't I?'

'Look, Roland wouldn't want me to take any risks with –'

'My safety?' Robyn shrugged. 'Well, he sent me here, didn't he? I'm just doing what I'm told.'

'Don't use me to score points against your dad,' said Niko, impatience in her voice. 'I have a serious job here.'

'Don't worry, I won't get in your way.'

'I'm not worried about that. I know how capable you are. You prove that every day.' Niko looked at her. 'Robyn, your mother was my best friend. I loved working with her; she was one of the best doctors I've ever met. She died and I couldn't save her – nobody could. But no way am I going to expose you to the same risks.'

'Those were risks Mum chose to take,' said Robyn quietly. 'I can choose them too. I want to.' She looked back at Niko more calmly. 'I guess you think I'm a spoiled brat, and I know I sulked about coming here. But now I'm here, I want to help.' When Niko still didn't answer, Robyn shrugged. 'Look, this is what Mum did, it's who she was. I . . . I'd appreciate it if you'd let me experience just a few hours of that today. Please?'

Niko looked weary but resigned. 'I know better than to argue,' she said at last. 'You know, you remind me of her so much.'

At that, Robyn felt a queasy mixture of emotions: sadness, envy, loss – and resentment. She sighed. Feelings for animals were so straightforward and positive in contrast – affection, happiness, trust, care. They didn't change; she understood them. Was it any wonder she never wanted to leave Crocodile Lodge?

Kiizu poked his head through the thick plastic partition. 'Is there a problem?'

'No problem,' Niko said, turning back to the pile of PPE. 'Robyn, I'll show you how to put everything on safely.'

'And I'll watch you both to double-check you follow every procedure,' said Kiizu. 'We can't allow this to spread any further.'

Robyn watched as Niko carefully donned layers of silicone and smart polymer cloth and plastic and glass.

'I always think of this stuff as my uniform.' Niko sterilised her hands, put the cloth gown over her clothes and sterilised her hands again. 'I'm like a soldier putting on her army fatigues, or a priest climbing into his robes.'

'You have to be a little of both to do this job,' Kiizu said.

Like Niko, Robyn put on a smartfibre medical mask and moulded it tightly over her nose and cheeks, puffing sharp breaths in and out to check the seal. Then she continued the routine of alternating sterilisations and protective layers over her hair, eyes, feet, the flexi-glass shield covering her face. Finally, she pulled the sleeves of her gown down over her wrists so the second set of synthetic polymer gloves would sit on top of the first set of gloves and her sleeves, forming a seal. She already felt hot and uncomfortable after just a few minutes, and took the time to murmur thanks to all the heroes who did this every day in the name of helping the sick.

'There! You're all set. Follow me, please.' Kiizu led them towards a meeting hall in the middle of the village. In her PPE, her breathing loud in her own ears, feeling insulated from the world, Robyn felt more like an astronaut than a medic.

Inside the hall, patients lay on beds behind plastic screens, some as still as corpses, some shuddering with hacking coughs. A woman in full PPE and with a tablet under one arm looked up and left a patient to come over.

'Dr Sabaya,' said Kiizu, 'this is Dr Niko Haart and . . .'

'Robyn Ballantyne,' Robyn said self-consciously.

'I'm Laia Sabaya.' The mask muffled her voice, but Robyn could tell the doctor was smiling from the way her eyes crinkled up. 'I've heard so much about you and your fine work, Dr Haart, so thank you for agreeing to join us here. Would you like to see a summary of the patients' conditions? Probably already out of date in some cases.' She took the stylus magnetised to the tablet and double-tapped one entry that had just started flashing orange. 'The young man over there – his vitals are dipping. Kiizu, would you?'

'On it,' Kiizu said, and with a nod to Robyn and Niko, hurried away to attend to the patient. Dr Sabaya handed the tablet to Niko.

Niko glanced over the report. 'It's torn through the village population, then.'

Dr Sabaya nodded. 'We're taking blood samples and sending them off for analysis, and we have teams working on contact tracing, but it's spreading fast. Would you and your assistant like to examine some of the patients?'

'I wouldn't *like* it, but it's why I'm . . . why *we're* here.' Niko scrunched up her eyes as much as she could in an attempt to show her smile beneath her mask. 'Lead on.'

Dr Sabaya took Robyn and Niko to a small dwelling a short walk away. It was one of the modern rondavel houses, with a polished concrete floor and an elegant thatched roof. There was air conditioning too, but Robyn couldn't feel it through her PPE.

'It's not the same as a sealed hospital room,' said Dr Sabaya with regret, 'but at least it's better than the meeting hall. This village simply doesn't have the facilities to provide isolated rooms for Patients Under Investigation. And the virus has spread so rapidly that we've not even been able to separate stable PUIs from those who are seriously ill.'

There were two people in the small house: an old woman lying very still in the bedroom and a man on a sofa bed in the living room, breathing hoarsely.

'Who are the patients here?' Robyn asked.

'Maggie Jacobs and her son, Stefan.' Dr Sabaya spoke like she was making introductions. 'It's her home; Stefan came to visit from Pretoria a few days ago. They both fell sick around the same time.'

'Did Stefan become infected here,' Niko wondered, 'or did he bring the infection with him?'

'Officially? Not certain.' Dr Sabaya shrugged. 'But my gut feeling? He brought it with him. Stefan's hardly been out since he arrived, but no one in the village was sick before he came.' She crossed to the old woman on the bed, who hadn't moved since they'd arrived. 'Oh, Maggie, we haven't lost you too, have we?'

Niko followed her, but Robyn held back. She wasn't squeamish; living on a reserve meant she'd seen death before. But she hoped she'd never get used to it. She thought of the young man in the meeting hall whose vital signs had dropped and wondered how he was.

'I'd put the time of death as maybe half an hour ago,' Niko said.

'She slipped away fairly peacefully, at least,' Dr Sabaya murmured. 'Most haven't had it so easy.'

As if in agreement, there was a groan from the living room. Niko strode over to the man on the sofa bed. Robyn followed with Dr Sabaya. He was sweating, hot with fever, and struggling to breathe.

'Could you take a blood sample?' Dr Sabaya looked between Robyn and Niko as if unsure which of them to ask. 'I'd best arrange for Maggie to be taken away.'

'Of course,' said Niko, as her new colleague hurried out. 'Robyn, could you open the medical kit, please?'

Robyn walked over to the white medical case on the coffee table and fumbled with the clasps. 'What do you need?'

'A gold vacutainer and a sharp,' Niko said, not looking

up from her patient. 'Uh, sorry, look for a blood collection tube with a yellow top and a hypodermic syringe, please.'

Robyn sifted clumsily through the contents until she found what was needed.

Niko took them from her without comment. 'Stefan?' She bent over him. 'Can you hear me, Stefan?'

The man just moaned again, corded muscles standing out in his neck as he strained to breathe. When Niko inserted the needle into his arm to take a blood sample, his eyes snapped open and fixed on Robyn. She was shocked to see that they were bright red.

Stefan coughed weakly and a dribble of blood oozed from the side of his mouth. 'I'm dying, aren't I?'

Robyn opened her mouth to reply but no words came out.

'We're going to help you, Stefan,' Niko said briskly. 'Robyn, get me another vacutainer. Any colour.'

Quickly, Robyn located a blue-capped tube and passed it over. Niko took a second blood sample.

'How many do you need to take?'

'The first one will go to the government lab,' Niko said. 'This one's for me. I want to examine it for myself. Back at SangoMed we have more up-to-date testing techniques. The more we know, and the sooner we know it, the better.' She withdrew the needle and handed the glass vials to Robyn. 'Can you put each of these in one of the plastic envelopes in the kit? If you seal them, I'll label them.' Niko went into the other room to see Maggie Jacobs. 'I'll just take a sample from her too, for comparison.'

'Right,' Robyn said, and got busy placing the tubes inside the envelopes.

Stefan stared after Niko. 'Ma?'

'I'm so sorry,' Robyn said. 'I'm sure the doctors did all they could.'

'It's me, isn't it?' Stefan gripped Robyn's wrist and squeezed hard. 'It's me who infected her, who killed her.'

'We don't know that,' said Robyn, trying to stay calm, keeping her voice low. 'We're trying to help you. Please, can you let go –'

'You can't help me. And people need to know why. They need to know what's happening.' Stefan reached under the covers, pulled out a folded piece of paper and pressed it into Robyn's gloved hand. 'There. There's nothing they can do to stop me now.'

'They? Who's they?' Robyn looked down at the paper and wondered if he was delirious, but she tucked it inside the back of her glove anyway. Then Stefan's coughing became more violent. An explosion of almost black blood erupted from his mouth, spraying over her sealed flex-glass face shield. Robyn let out a sharp cry of shock and disgust and backed away. Niko hurried out from the other room, saw the gore and grabbed a sterile cloth from the medical kit.

'Here,' she said, starting to clean Robyn's face shield.

'I'm all right,' Robyn said, pulling the cloth from Niko to finish the job herself. 'You should see to him.'

But Stefan was lying still, red tears streaming down his contorted face. Niko checked him. 'No pulse.'

'What could do this to all these people?' Robyn wondered aloud.

'We'll find out,' Niko said. Working quickly and carefully, she finished wiping down Robyn's face shield using a strong disinfectant spray. Then she labelled the blood samples and pushed one of them into a pouch in her protective trousers beneath her gown.

Robyn was about to tell her about the paper Stefan had given her when Dr Sabaya came in. The woman's shoulders slumped as she took in Stefan and the blood-spattered bed. 'So. We've lost him too.'

Niko nodded. 'I'm sorry.' She picked up the remaining sample from the table. 'Here's his blood sample.'

Dr Sabaya took the sample without thanks or comment. 'We'll need a full clean-up crew in here.'

Robyn shivered and turned away, leaving Dr Sabaya and Niko to discuss the next steps. She saw a small biohazard bag on a table and thought of the note that Stefan had been so desperate to pass her.

With only a little fumbling, she managed to take off the outermost of her two left gloves with the note still tucked inside and shoved it in the bag. Then she sealed the bag and slipped it into the pouch in her trousers, just as Niko had. She glanced back, afraid she'd been seen. But the two women were still deep in conversation.

Now Robyn wished she'd taken the time to read the note. A tingle travelled through her.

What did the message say?

4

Dawn broke hard outside Ralph's bedroom windows, showing a sky like blue steel. Roland knocked on his bedroom door and shouted threats to leave him behind – he and Xai were ready to go now. Ralph dressed hastily between gulps of thick Jungle Oats sweetened with a spoonful of Cape gooseberry jam. Within fifteen minutes he was jumping into the back of the truck. Xai started the electric engine and they pulled away.

As the truck rumbled through the sprawling forest of yellowwood and ironwood, Ralph eyed the carefully stored rifles and mesh nets they used to contain dangerous wounded predators. He felt a thrill of excitement. Whatever it was that had chased the lion and springbok, at least they had the tools now to deal with it. If they found it.

'Two questions,' Ralph said. 'Where are we going? And can I carry more than just a tranq gun?'

'We don't know what we're going to find yet,' Roland said.

'Dad, you know I can handle a rifle,' Ralph said. 'I've got the trophies to prove it.' Under his dad and Xai's watchful eyes, he'd been firing a Winchester Model 70 since he was six years old and had won dozens of target practice tournaments.

'Firing in a competition with the range master watching and firing at big game when you're exposed and in danger are very different things,' Roland went on. Then he sighed. 'But I know you understand and appreciate all the safety procedures.'

'Because I learned from the best,' Ralph said.

'All right, no need to kiss butt.' His dad gave him a sideways look. 'You can take a rifle. But you're not to fire unless Xai or I give the signal. Not at *anything*. Got it?'

'I hear you,' Ralph said, and he meant it. He felt proud that his dad was trusting him with live rounds at fourteen, but also queasy at the thought of what he might have to fire at.

'And as for where we're going, we're heading to the shallow bank, north of the Girdle,' Roland said. The Girdle was what they called a narrow stretch of forest that cut through the shrubland near the river. 'We spotted the amphibious craft not far from there.'

'That's where the elephant was making for too,' Ralph recalled, with a pang of concern.

As they rounded the Girdle, the river came into view through a straggle of mopane trees. Ralph glimpsed grey and crimson – and his stomach turned.

Ahead of them, surrounded by a crowd of feasting flies, was a gruesome, mutilated mass that had once been a magnificent bull elephant. The enormous head had almost been torn away from the bloodied body, the tusks curving up like monuments to the ruins of the hollowed flesh below.

'What happened?' Ralph whispered.

'An elephant's the largest land animal in the world,' Xai said quietly. 'And something has torn it apart.'

Repulsed but transfixed by the elephant's butchered corpse, Ralph got down from the truck and tentatively walked closer. Roland followed his son, spraying a pheromone spray into the air, luring the swarm of flies safely away from the corpse. 'We're *definitely* not dealing with poachers.'

'They would never leave the ivory behind,' Ralph reasoned.

'And just look at these bite marks,' said Xai. 'They've scissored through the hide like it was paper.'

'Crocodile bites?' Ralph suggested, then caught himself. 'No. They're too big!'

'I don't know.' Roland moved forward to take pictures of the bites with his satellite phone. 'It *does* look like a croc – but it would have to be a huge one.'

'With jaws something like two metres long,' Xai said. 'It's hard to say because there's so much swelling in the wounds, but the teeth don't seem to match. A croc would have maybe twenty teeth each side of its upper and lower jaws. This looks closer to thirty.'

As always, Ralph was impressed by Xai's insight, but not surprised; Xai's name meant 'eye' in Khoe, the South African language family. It suited him well. Ralph valued every opportunity to watch Xai at work.

'So, something big with too many teeth,' said Ralph, nervously gazing around. The riverbank was a flat, broad stretch of reddish soil and rocks, with foxtail buffalo grass and guinea grass that would attract grazing animals. The ground was churned up from the struggle between the elephant and whatever had killed it, but it was hard to make out any proper tracks.

'I'd like to know how the intruders are linked to this,' said Xai.

'I'd like to know how Josef Gerhard is involved,' Roland retorted. 'With the amphibious craft, the intruders, the murder of this poor elephant – all of it!'

'We don't know that Gerhard *is* involved,' Xai argued.

'How about we try to find some concrete proof that he is?' said Ralph. 'Something we can confront him with?'

Roland nodded. 'We'll search along the riverbank. Ralph, you and Xai go upriver. Start from the sandbanks at Boulder Point – an amphib craft couldn't help leaving tracks if it's crossed there. We'll work towards each other and meet in the middle.'

Xai nodded. 'The sand is soft; we may yet find prints.'

'Be careful on your own, Dad,' Ralph said mock-sternly. 'You won't have me around to watch your back.'

Roland forced a smile. 'Just keep the little rogue safe, OK?'

Xai smiled at the use of his nickname. Roland's Special Forces brigade had given it to him years back after he'd braved enemy lines in battle, against orders, and saved a dozen lives; Ralph knew that Xai was proud of the term and what it symbolised.

Ralph got back in the truck. Xai drove along the riverbank path for a few hundred metres, his posture relaxed but eyes and ears sharp as he scanned the landscape around him.

Soon they reached Boulder Point. As Xai parked up, Ralph noted with a mix of relief and disappointment that the muddy sand was undisturbed, suggesting that whatever had intruded hadn't ventured this far.

Xai slung a precision rifle over his shoulder. 'We'll work our way downriver.' He hesitated, then loaded four rounds into a Model 70 and passed the rifle to Ralph. 'I don't know what kind of animal made those teeth marks. We should be ready for anything.'

Ralph accepted the Winchester with a nod of thanks. As they walked away from the truck he held it pointing towards the ground, his finger off the trigger, as he'd been taught. The background sound of birds and beasts seemed muted here by the river, and the scrunch of their footsteps sounded unnaturally loud.

'So, if a crocodile didn't kill that elephant,' Ralph said, 'what did?'

Xai half-smiled. 'I try to keep an open mind. Believe in a hunch and your mind may make patterns where they don't exist – or miss clues that do.'

Ralph nodded and looked around. Perhaps twenty metres ahead, a piece of timber stuck drunkenly out of the long grass by the river. His first thought was that it would have made a good marker for them to begin their search. His second was that it shouldn't be there at all. It wasn't a tree stump. It was more like a post protruding from a bare patch in the grassy bank.

'Xai, look,' Ralph said. 'What's that?'

Xai marched over to investigate. Ralph had to run to keep up. As they got closer, Ralph saw black stripes near the top of the post and dark marks on the ground around it. He wondered if Xai had spotted them immediately, hence his haste to get there.

The black stripes proved to be fabric. 'That's the same stuff the springbok's collar was made from,' Ralph realised.

'And this is fresh blood.' Xai had crouched to scan the ground more closely. 'Look at these marks.'

Ralph already was. 'A springbok was here.'

Xai gazed up at him. 'More closely, Ralph.'

'The prints . . . they're slightly different sizes.' Ralph nodded. 'A *lot* of springbok tied up to this post – but why?'

'I think I know.' Xai straightened up. 'Have you ever seen forest rangers use a goat as bait to draw out a rogue leopard?'

'I've heard of that happening,' Ralph said. 'Are you saying these intruders came in by boat and tied up a bunch of springbok to draw something out?'

'And you found one of the lucky ones that managed to get away,' said Xai. 'As for whatever it was they were trying to lure . . .'

Ralph shook his head grimly. 'Whatever freak of nature it is, I hope they caught it.'

'Perhaps they did,' Xai said. He turned to the river's edge and began scouting for tracks. 'It would explain why so much of the bull's carcass was left behind. Either that, or . . .'

Ralph swallowed. 'Or?'

Xai's look sent chills down Ralph's back. 'Or it wasn't killing because it was hungry. It was killing for sport.' Xai went back to methodically scanning the reeds and marshy ground.

Ralph attempted to do the same in a different area. The bank looked smooth, almost as though freshly raked over, but the reeds at the water's edge had been crushed by something. An amphibious craft? They must have landed nearby to place the stake and tie up the springbok . . .

Then again, perhaps the creature the intruders had been trying to lure out had emerged here.

A sandflat a few metres from the river's edge showed signs of a scuffle. Cautiously, Ralph stepped into the shallow water and started to wade across to investigate. But he froze as he caught movement in the water. Something dark, spreading slowly like smoke.

Blood, he realised. *Get out.*

He hesitated: should he turn and make his way quietly back to shore or press onwards to the sandflat? But then something burst up from the water. Ralph shrieked as vice-like jaws clamped around his left leg. He saw the creature's dark, narrowed eyes above a long snout and raised his gun, but the creature jerked its head wildly. Ralph lost his balance, falling into the water. The beast released Ralph's leg and Ralph propelled himself back to shore, scrambling onto the sand and turning to fire into the water. The recoil jarred his shoulder and the dark bulk of the creature jerked beneath the surface of the water.

'Ralph?' Xai shouted, pelting towards him. 'Are you all right?'

'I . . . I don't even . . .' Ralph couldn't form the words, frightened to see what damage had been done to his calf. He imagined the flesh hanging from the bone. But when he looked, there were only deep red welts and bruising; the skin hadn't even been broken. 'I'm fine.'

'Thank God.' As Xai arrived, the dead creature floated to the surface. It was a hefty-looking crocodile. Ralph shuddered when he saw the hole he'd drilled through the beast's skull. He put the rifle down. Xai waded in and gripped the croc's jaws, pulling them open.

'You were lucky, Ralph,' he said. 'This monster's lost most of his teeth.'

'What?' Ralph got up warily to see. 'How did that happen?'

'Let's take a closer look.' Xai started to drag the beast's body up onto the sandflat. Ralph helped him. There was a deep gash in the croc's side.

'He was bleeding out,' Xai said. 'Well done, Ralph. That wasn't just a good clean shot, it was a mercy killing. You've spared him a long, slow death.'

'What did this to him?' Ralph breathed.

'The gash . . . could be tusks, or claws? As for the teeth, I can only think he bit down hard on something that was too tough.'

'Like the hull of a boat?'

'No. That might leave some teeth broken. His have been torn clear out of the gums.' Xai looked pensive. 'It's as if he attacked something with a very tough hide. Something that fought back.'

'The same something that our human intruders are looking for,' Ralph mused quietly.

'Yes. I'm amazed he had any strength or will left to attack you. Must have been acting out of terror.'

'I know just how he felt.' Ralph looked at Xai. 'How long since he was injured?'

'Can't be too long ago, or the croc would already be dead.' Xai came back out of the water and placed a hand on Ralph's shoulder. 'If you're up to it, help me with that stake? We should take it to show your father.'

Ralph helped Xai heave the wooden post out of the blood-soaked ground and carry it back to the truck. Ralph shuddered again at the strange stillness in the air. There should have been birdsong, the small rustlings of animals in the trees and grasses; it was as if all nature had fled the horror here. He was glad of the comforting electric hum of the vehicle as it rattled along the bumpy track and away from the crocodile's body on the riverbank.

Xai parked, and Ralph ran to tell his father all that had happened. He took care to play down the ferocity of the croc attack, not wanting to be grounded on the spot for his own protection.

Roland studied Ralph's bruised leg like a forensic expert. 'I'm glad something took out the croc's teeth before it could take *you* out.' He straightened. 'We'd better alert all rangers to keep a look out for whatever did this.'

'It must be a giant of a predator,' said Ralph.

Roland nodded. 'Any and all other wildlife is at risk. Rangers too. We have to capture this beast and fast.'

Ralph echoed his father's nod. He thought of the *thing* he'd glimpsed chasing the lion yesterday. It stood to reason that the same creature was responsible for attacking the

43

croc. 'But if some giant predator was living in the river, surely we would have spotted it before – or the remains of its prey, anyway?'

'Not necessarily,' said Xai. 'A beast that size would have to cruise a huge river territory to find enough to eat. It may have targeted Gerhard's reserve too.'

'Someone certainly did,' said Ralph. 'The springbok we found, the one that escaped from the stake – it was Gerhard's. Whoever was in the amphibious craft could've stolen it from his reserve!'

'Why take the risk of stealing springbok from Gerhard and then come into our territory too?' Roland argued. 'Unless this all *started* in Gerhard's reserve. Whatever they were after got away from them and got through the river gate between his land and ours.'

'So they had to trespass here in search of it?' Xai nodded thoughtfully. 'Gerhard must really want to capture that creature.'

'To hunt it and mount it on the wall, knowing him,' Ralph said gloomily.

'I'm going to contact Gerhard,' Roland announced. 'Xai, will you take care of the elephant's body?'

'Of course,' said Xai. 'I'll radio for a couple of rangers. We'll take the croc too; treat their remains with the dignity they deserve.'

Roland smiled sadly. 'Thanks, little rogue.'

'What about me?' said Ralph. 'What do you want me to do?'

'Rest that leg,' said Roland, and held up his hands when

Ralph started to protest. 'No arguments. I'll drive you home ready for your lessons.' He forced a smile. 'It's not so bad. VanRok Security is sending a tech team out this afternoon and Luke's coming with them. I'm sure he'll look in on you.'

Ralph half-smiled. Luke was a few years older than him but acted a few years younger. Mr Van Rok had high hopes for his eldest son to work his way up through the company, but it was no secret that Luke preferred playing video games to playing businessman. 'They're here fast. You only called them last night,' Ralph noted.

'I offered Van Rok a free stay with us if he could get someone here in twenty-four hours,' said Roland. 'Although I imagine Luke is always available at short notice!'

'Available for gaming while he sends the others out to work,' Ralph said with a smile.

'That one you've been playing might feel a little too close to home today,' Xai said wryly. 'What was it?'

'*Predasaur*,' Ralph answered, climbing into the truck. He'd been telling Xai about his progress on the super-realistic game only a couple of nights ago. *Predasaur* had been a top-selling game for the past couple of years, and was famous for its ultra-real graphics and cutscenes – with the vivid deaths of both hunters and animals. He and Robyn both played it: a first-person shooter which prided itself on historical accuracy alongside full-on adventure. And he knew what Xai meant: one of the bosses in *Predasaur* was a huge crocodile-like beast that roamed the waterways causing carnage. It was based on a creature that had lived in West Africa a hundred million years ago, during the Cretaceous period.

Ralph was dragged from his thoughts by a squawk from Xai's radio. He'd called Carol, a park warden, for back-up.

'Can't come yet,' Carol said over the static. 'Emergency.'

'What emergency?' Roland snapped.

Carol hesitated. 'It's the lion. Jari . . . he's been attacked.'

Ralph sat bolt upright, feeling sick. 'I told you I saw a lion being chased!' he cried, already imagining how Robyn would feel. She'd pretty much raised Jari and Sabal single-handed. 'Is he dead? Is he – ?'

Roland waved him sharply into silence.

'He's badly hurt,' Carol said. 'His right flank's slashed to ribbons. Wounds all over his body like nothing I've ever seen. We're patching him up and we've radioed for the vet to come in from Pretoria. She reckons it'll take a couple of hours, minimum.'

Roland swore. 'We'd best not try to move Jari till the vet gets here. Build a shelter to keep the sun off him. I'll join you shortly.' He ended the call and shot Ralph a look sharp enough to cut. 'Looks like you were right last night. You did see a lion being chased by . . . something.' He shook his head. 'Well, whatever it might be, it's not safe out here. You're going home.'

Ralph didn't argue this time. He was thinking of the crocodile creature from *Predasaur*. Its name sprang to Ralph's mind with the same suddenness of a mantrap closing its jaws: sarcosuchus, a massive, ancient super-croc, twelve metres long, with jaws as big as a man. It was the only beast he could imagine being able to swallow half a dozen springbok whole, then tear apart an elephant, a lion and a giant croc for fun.

But that's impossible, Ralph told himself. A prehistoric monster emerging from the water and tearing apart the wildlife? It was crazy.

Wasn't it?

5

Robyn spent all day with Niko in the infected village, helping with everything from making patients comfortable to taking notes for post-mortems on the dead. She thought she might pass out from the heat inside all her gear. Her face felt numb from where the shield pushed into her skin, but she was grateful for the protection: over half the people in the village were showing signs of symptoms now.

At five o'clock, Robyn went outside to take a break. She was trying not to shake, and felt more tired than she could ever remember.

'Hey.' Niko came up beside her. 'I think your shift has ended.'

Robyn looked at her. 'What about yours?'

'Mine too,' Niko said. 'I've done all I can here for the moment.'

I don't know how you do this, Robyn wanted to say. *I don't know how my mum did this: cared for others so willingly.* In the PPE Robyn felt like a robot, cut off from the world around her. To be tracking an animal, clear-eyed, with the tingle of sun on her skin: that was her world. To breathe in the musky scents of the bush, the fragrance of flowers and animals, was as natural to her as breathing. But to nurse the sick, cocooned in a plastic gown, to watch people die to the background buzz of the air pump in sealed treatment rooms and the whoosh of each purified breath in her ears . . . After hours of enduring it her throat was raw, her eyes were red with tears, and she felt like a predator trapped in a tiny cage. *So how do you do it?* she wanted to ask. But if she did, then Niko would know she was impressed, and Robyn didn't want to give her the satisfaction.

'What do you think's going to happen?' she asked as casually as she could. 'I mean, what can you do?'

Niko shrugged. 'I've urged Dr Sabaya to contact the Department of Health and demand that a strict lockdown be put in force, not just here but in all the villages in the area. They need more staff and mobile decontamination units to keep them safe too. And once she's put in the request, I can follow up and offer extra resources to the government from SangoMed – even if I have to call in on the Department of Health in person and make a nuisance of myself until someone listens.' She paused, then sighed and turned to Robyn. 'Come on, I'll show you how to get out of your PPE safely.'

'We're leaving then?'

'Yes. We're the lucky ones. Anyway, I can do more back in my office.'

Niko led the way to the doffing section of the tent. Robyn watched and learned as, quickly but carefully, Niko removed and disinfected her PPE. Niko took out the bio-waste bag with the blood sample. Robyn realised there was no way she could smuggle out her own bag containing Stefan's note and her gloves, so she decided to style it out.

As soon as she took it out of her pocket, Niko looked concerned. 'What's that? What did you take from in there?'

'That man – Stefan. He gave me a note.' Robyn shrugged.

Niko looked shocked. 'What did it say?'

'I didn't have a chance to read it,' Robyn admitted. 'But he said that people need to know why. They need to know what's happening.'

'We should get it to Dr Sabaya,' Niko said, picking up the bio-waste bag and putting it in her rucksack with her own. 'Stefan was her patient.'

Robyn frowned. 'Can't I see what it says?'

'It's not our business,' Niko said. 'Anyway, it will need to be opened in a sterile, controlled environment. Robyn, you took a huge, unnecessary risk, taking off your gloves like that unsupervised.'

'I had the other pair on underneath,' Robyn protested. 'I get that Dad would never talk to you again if anything happened to me, but chill, I'm fine. You don't have to worry about another Ballantyne dying on you.'

'Just get in the shower,' Niko said quietly. 'We have to decontaminate.'

Robyn did so without further comment. She knew that her dig had been uncalled for, that she should apologise. But the same stubbornness that kept her standing after her long ordeal kept her quiet.

The shower did little to revive her; the water was tepid

and low-pressure and she had to stay in it for fifteen minutes to be sure that she was fully decontaminated.

When Robyn emerged, Niko was just completing decontamination in the next cubicle. Outside, over the hissing of the pipes as the hot water boiler cooled down, she could hear the throb of engines and the squeal of brakes. *Reinforcements*, Robyn thought with relief.

She dried herself and dressed, and was just slipping on her shoes when she heard raised voices outside. People were shouting and someone was crying. Robyn felt a pang of pity and a deep, deep tiredness. Someone else fading away, she supposed. Helpless relatives yelling at doctors in their frustration. She'd seen it all today. The quiet village had become a war zone.

Robyn heard Niko's shower switch off. She was about to leave the area to avoid any further awkward encounters, but before she did she took Niko's clothes out of the locker and laid them out for her. Then she stepped outside. The warm breeze ruffled her wet hair. She could hear more shouting.

A man was yelling, 'Let go of me!'

And then Robyn heard Dr Sabaya. 'I need to see proof of your authority. Your credentials. Evacuation orders –'

There was a crash. Someone cried out. Dr Sabaya didn't speak again.

Feeling uneasy, Robyn went back inside the tent to tell Niko, who was dressed and swinging her backpack onto her shoulder, what had happened. She smiled at Robyn.

Her smile fell when Kiizu came racing into the tent, minus his protective headgear. He was sweating and his eyes were wide.

'Did you hear –' Robyn began.

'Quiet,' Kiizu hissed. 'You must hide.' He opened the door of her locker and all but bundled Robyn inside, then grabbed Niko's arm. 'Both of you.'

'What's going on?' Niko cried.

'*Quiet*, I said. And hurry.' Kiizu looked behind him, terrified. 'Soldiers – they came from nowhere. They want us in the meeting hall.'

Robyn frowned. 'What, the doctors?'

'Everyone,' said Kiizu. He grabbed a towel and wiped it around the cubicle's wet floor. 'I think they saw me come in.' He rubbed the towel over his hair to give the impression he'd just stepped out of the shower, then wrapped it round his neck. 'You have to hide, then when it's safe get out of here. Get help.'

'Look, slow down,' Niko said. 'Surely these are just first responders?'

'Not a sound,' Kiizu warned. Something in his eyes chilled Robyn to the core, and she found herself shrinking into her locker. Niko did the same. Kiizu closed the locker doors on them, just as there was a clatter outside. Robyn heard him run towards the exit.

Through the crack between her locker door and the one above, Robyn saw two figures in dark green hazmat suits barge into the tent, each holding an automatic weapon. Soldiers, just like he said. Kiizu skidded to a stop.

'Ah, Doctor,' said the man closest to Kiizu. His voice rattled through a speaker built into his plastic helmet-hood. 'What are you doing here?'

'Decon,' Kiizu said calmly, dropping the wet towel on the floor. 'Starting another shift.'

'Well, you're needed. There's an urgent briefing in the hall.' The soldier looked around. 'Anyone else here with you?'

Kiizu shook his head. 'No, everyone's flat out. Well, I guess I'll join your briefing in the hall, then –'

'Get back, Kiizu!' Dr Sabaya burst into the tent, her face bruised and bloody. 'They're impostors!'

The soldier raised his rifle stock and brought it down on Dr Sabaya's forehead. Robyn shrank back in horror.

'No!' Kiizu shouted. But the other soldier karate-chopped the doctor's neck. With a choked cry, Kiizu crumpled and fell.

Robyn bit her lip and hugged herself to stop shaking. If she made a noise, she knew she'd be caught.

The man who'd hit Kiizu stared down at the fallen doctors. 'They should stay sleeping till this is all over,' he said. 'I'll load them onto gurneys, say they're sick.'

His friend nodded. 'We don't want any more trouble, but if anyone tries to give it – remember, no bullets. Bullets could be found when the law go over what's left of the bodies.'

The two men picked up Kiizu and Dr Sabaya and left. Robyn released a long, shuddering breath. She almost screamed when Niko opened her locker door, her face grave, her eyes full of fear. 'Are you OK?' she said.

'What's happening?' Robyn demanded.

'I don't know. But we have to get help, like Kiizu said.'

Robyn nodded. 'He risked his life to keep us safe. They both did.' Quietly, her heart banging in her ears, she got out of the locker, crept to the tent flap and looked out. No one was nearby. The village seemed deserted. She looked back at Niko. 'Are we on any visitor lists? Will the soldiers be looking for us?'

'There wasn't time to sign in,' Niko said. 'I guess the soldiers could have found our boat at the jetty, if they're trying to seal the area. They could trace that to SangoMed, maybe.'

'But not straight to you?' Robyn queried, and was relieved when Niko shook her head. 'Then maybe the soldiers think they've found everyone.'

'Yes,' Niko whispered slowly. 'Yes, of course. You're right. Sorry, I'm not thinking clearly.'

'Let's get to the boat,' Robyn said.

Niko nodded.

They crept outside together. The sultry night air revived Robyn: the wind stirred her spirit and fear sharpened her senses, just as they would any other animal. This was like searching for wildlife at night. You had to move quietly, stealthily . . .

And you needed luck.

Robyn's luck seemed to hold. She and Niko kept to the cover of the medical trailers as much as they could, jogging along the path towards the jetty where their boat was moored. There seemed an unnatural stillness about the area, as if the world was holding its breath. There was no noise from the village – none of the cheerful sounds of everyday life like children playing or roosters crowing. Just a sickly smell of death and decay.

'Get on board,' Niko hissed. 'I'll untie us.'

Robyn was trembling as she got into the boat, but after Niko had unfastened the mooring rope and climbed aboard, she picked up an oar and used it to push off from the jetty. Not daring to start the engine, they let the current take the boat and drifted downriver.

'I can't believe we made it out,' Niko whispered.

'We're not safe yet,' Robyn muttered as she heard the angry buzz of a helicopter. She froze as she glimpsed its shadow against the deep indigo sky. It was flying without lights.

Then a huge explosion shook the world. Robyn was thrown onto her back and Niko was almost tossed overboard. Birds and bats rose from the thick bushes either side of the river as a mass of black smoke billowed up from behind the tree cover, chased by the lick of orange flames.

'The village,' Robyn breathed.

'It has its own generator,' Niko said, her face frozen in fright. 'It must've exploded. Or been blown up deliberately.'

Robyn could hardly take it in: the sick, the dead, the living . . . the entire community. They had been herded into the main hall to be 'briefed' on the situation. 'Do you think everyone's dead? The whole village?'

'I don't know. But that has to be why the soldiers came,' said Niko. 'They must be trying to hide the virus. But why? Who gave the orders?'

Robyn thought of the note in Niko's bag, and Stefan's last words. '*People need to know why,*' she repeated. 'That's what Stefan Jacobs told me. *There's nothing they can do to stop me now.*'

'These murderers have had a damn good try,' Niko muttered. She checked that the bio-waste envelope was still safely in her bag, then she wiped the tears from her eyes, primed the engine and yanked the starter cord. Robyn felt a glimmer of relief as the boat sped away, but the smoke from the explosion followed them overhead, like a black hand closing slowly over the world.

6

The bushveld was rimmed with gold as the sun slowly sank towards its sleep. Oblivious to what was happening to his sister, Ralph stood in the gardens of the Lodge, target shooting with his Mauser M98 Magnum.

He looked through the scope at the tin can on top of the wall from a hundred metres away, his finger gently cradling the trigger. His leg still ached, but not enough to break his concentration. For Ralph, shooting wasn't just the perfect antidote to long, dull hours of online schooling; it was the best way he knew to clear his head of clutter, to push worries from his mind. He got a real buzz from his increasing mastery of target shooting – plus, it helped him to play *Predasaur* in Expert Mode – the aiming systems were so sensitive, the skills required so precise. He'd been playing with Luke van Rok that afternoon and crushed him with a top-ranking kill-death ratio. Luke couldn't get past the Eurasian cave lion guarding the end of Battlespace Three, whereas Ralph was already free-roaming the land beyond.

He only wished all hunting was virtual, unfeeling animations the only victims.

As he got ready for the shot, he thought back to his ancestors: rugged people in rugged times who did things their own way in defiance of the commonplace. His great-great-great-great-grandfather, Zouga Ballantyne, had a son called Ralph and a sister named Robyn; the names had been passed down through the Ballantyne family, synonymous with courage and resourcefulness. Zouga had written a memoir of his wild life at the frontiers of civilisation in the nineteenth century, which Ralph had read many times. Zouga's peers had labelled him reckless and irresponsible – an Adventurist.

Ralph loved to imagine his ancestor back in those days – surviving on his skill, wits and luck. Roland was adding his own chapters to the memoir, recounting his adventurist exploits back in the Special Forces: the friendships forged and enemies made, the long shots that paid off . . . The book was part of the family, passed down through the generations, growing with the years.

A story that will never end, Roland had called it.

Ralph dreamed of one day earning his name and being labelled an Adventurist himself, weaving his own wild encounters into words and writing them down for others to marvel at.

A nearby bird rasped its call, bringing Ralph back to reality. He checked his aim. Instinct and ability dovetailed as he squeezed the trigger . . .

The tin can jumped but didn't fall. He'd only clipped it.

Ralph lowered the rifle and took a deep breath. He'd made that shot dozens of times. But he knew why he was off his game. The slaughter of the old elephant and the attack on poor Jari had shaken him deeply. He was dreading his sister getting home, knowing the shock she'd feel.

Lucky for her she's been held up with Niko, he thought. *Better a boring day doing work experience than being here and going through all this.*

Ralph fired the last round, this time blowing the can off its perch. As the echoes of the shot faded, he heard his dad call to him across the lawn. 'Ralph! Have you heard from your sister?'

'No. What's wrong?' Ralph's stomach pinched at his dad's urgent tone and grave expression. 'Is it Jari?'

'Jari's been moved to the recovery pens. He's hanging in there,' Roland said. 'But I'm worried about Robyn and Niko. They're coming in now. Something's happened, but Niko won't say what until they're here.'

'What, like they had a row, you mean?'

'No. Something big.' Roland shook his head and stared off into the distance. 'The VanRok team's still busy. And Xai's fitting a bigger engine on the cabin cruiser in case the new security set-up finds any more amphibious craft on our waters.'

'Have you managed to get hold of Gerhard?' Ralph asked.

'No. His personal assistant claims he's in Europe on important business and can't be disturbed.' Roland's voice was hard. 'So I tried his head of security – a thug called Shrinker – and asked if they'd had any trouble. He said no. So then I asked how one of his boss's springbok had ended up in our territory, and he said that was impossible. Either we had a faulty chip reader or we were trying to smear Josef Gerhard's good name.' He was clearly set to continue his tirade when his satellite phone chimed. He snatched it from his pocket and stared at the message on the screen. 'Robyn says they've just parked up. And that we should turn on the news right now. It's about Gauda.'

'Where?' Ralph asked.

'It's a village out in the bush.' Roland tapped some keys on the phone. His frown deepened. 'It . . . *was* a village. Gauda's been razed to the ground. An explosion, massive fires. Hundreds dead.'

Ralph stared at him, barely able to process the tragedy. It wouldn't just be people, of course, but animals would also be caught in the blaze. 'What caused the fires?'

'The old solar generator went up. An accident, they're saying.'

'They're lying!' shouted Robyn, who had just burst into sight. She seemed close to tears. 'It's a cover-up. It was no accident.'

Ralph and Roland rushed over to her and she clutched them. Ralph gasped as she squeezed him tightly.

'What the hell happened?' Roland asked.

'We saw what they did. We were there.' Robyn was shaking. 'We *know*.'

Niko came up behind her. 'Come inside,' she said quietly. 'Roland, we all need to talk.'

Two hours later, Ralph still felt cold after the story Niko and Robyn had reported. A killer virus, murdering soldiers – it was like something out of a movie. He felt sorry for Robyn for having gone through so much.

He hated to admit it, even to himself, but he also felt a stab of envy at what she'd experienced. She could call herself an Adventurist now, and write her own chapter in Zouga Ballantyne's book, adding her adventures to the exploits of her forebears. And what had he done? Been bitten by a toothless old croc and missed some potshots at a tin can.

But Ralph had seen Robyn's face when Dad had told her the bad news about Jari, and suddenly he wasn't so eager to put himself in Robyn's shoes.

He watched her now, kneeling in the recovery pen, her hands against the bars of Jari's cage. The lion was lying still, reeking of the chlorhexidine solution that had been used to clean his injuries. He was too weak to eat or drink, so an IV drip fed him fluids. Jari's injuries were covered in wet-to-dry bandages – long lengths of gauze moistened with antiseptic and allowed to dry on the wound. The idea was that, as the dressing dried, the dead skin beneath would stick to the bandage and pull free when removed. The problem was, it was hard to see where Jari's wounds ended and healthy skin began.

'I don't think he'll ever hunt again.' Robyn's words were whispered, but they filled the space. 'The vet had to remove his tail, and without that for balance and ballast . . . even if he had both ears still . . . he'll need care for the rest of his life.'

Ralph groped around for something comforting to say, but came up empty. She was clearly feeling Jari's pain. There was a real bond between Robyn and the animals she looked after, particularly those she had helped to rear.

'So, when d'you find out what this guy Stefan's note says?' Ralph asked.

Robyn shrugged. 'Maybe never. It has to be handled carefully. Niko will need to open it somewhere safe.'

'She and your dad are looking at a letter right now in the examination room.' Luke van Rok sauntered into the pens: a tall, well-built seventeen-year-old with long blond hair, he had the air of a surfer dude just in from the beach. 'Hey, Ralph, I cannot let today's defeat lie. And since I'm staying in the staff quarters tonight, as there's no way we'll finish all the stuff your dad's got us doing, let's have a rematch tomorrow, OK?'

'Wait a minute.' Robyn rose from Jari's cage. 'Dad and Niko are looking at it now?'

'Looks that way, Rob. I was checking through the new camera feeds, and, yeah!' Luke held up his tablet. 'There they are.'

Sure enough, Niko, wearing vet scrubs, was using tweezers to open the bloodied paper while Roland Ballantyne watched through the observation window.

Ralph raised an eyebrow. 'So, you're spying on your employer?'

'I wouldn't use those words. I'm just testing the systems.' Luke turned off the screen and grinned. 'Now, are we on for a rematch or not?'

Ralph couldn't help but smile. 'I'll whup your butt anytime you like.'

'Tomorrow morning is fine,' Luke informed him. 'Meanwhile, I need to finish the last job of the night. We're just gonna mount another camera on the roof here. Is that cool?'

'Using power tools?' Robyn shook her head. 'No. These animals need quiet and rest.'

'Ah, that's fair. I'll tell Rameet to go in by hand.' Luke cast a sad glance at Jari in the cage. 'Heard about your lion, Rob. Sorry. Bummer.'

'Thanks, Luke,' said Robyn quietly. 'His name is Jari.'

'Got it. Sorry, Jari. Glad to see some of the lions are doing OK, though.' Luke swiped on the tablet again and held it up for her to see. 'Look at this mighty dude.'

'Sabal!' Robyn rose and rushed over to Luke, all but snatching the tablet from him. 'Oh, there you are.'

'Thank God he's OK,' Ralph said.

'But for how long?' Robyn handed the tablet back to Luke with a grateful nod. 'What if that *thing* out there gets Sabal too, or another elephant, or . . .'

'There's no sign of any jumbo croc out there now.' Luke crossed to the springbok's pen. 'Anyway, this little antelope looks fine. What's he called?'

'*She* is a springbok and she doesn't have a name,' said Ralph. 'She's not even ours. There's a chip in her, says she's property of Josef Gerhard.'

'Yeah?' Luke pulled out his phone and tapped on an app. 'Let's try a VanRok chip reader. Digs a little deeper. Maybe her name's in the metadata.'

Ralph and Robyn swapped a look. 'I doubt Gerhard gave

her one. He must have a thousand springbok in his park,' Ralph said.

'So why's most of the data on this chip encrypted then?' Luke smirked at them. 'This little springbok must have something to hide. Wanna find out what?'

Ralph frowned. 'Can you break the code on that thing?'

'Security's the family business, bruh,' said Luke, tapping away at a program. 'It's just a shame Dad expects me to work my way up from tea boy and pays me a pittance. I wish I could work for a big company like Gerhard Industries and earn some real money.'

'Gerhard is scum,' Robyn said automatically.

'Maybe so. But he's *rich* scum.' Luke went on tapping. 'Sorry, it shouldn't take long. VanRok software's pretty much plug-and-play. That's how come we've grown so fast, because we don't keep the customer waiting. We get –' There was a quiet chime. 'Results.'

'You're in?' Ralph said, impressed.

'Yeah. But there's nothing very interesting.' Luke pushed his blond fringe out of his eyes. 'Batch number 2341. Fifth-generation clone. Date of manufacture . . . four days ago.'

'The chip's only just gone in, then,' Ralph mused. 'What does "fifth-generation clone" mean?'

Luke shrugged. 'No idea, bruh.'

'A clone is a duplicate copy,' said Robyn.

'I know you can get cloning software to copy an entire hard drive and all its settings,' Luke said. 'I guess the chip's settings could've been cloned if they were putting them into lots of animals.'

'What else is hidden in the tag?' Robyn pressed him.

'Copyright stuff about the chip software – property of Q-Base Holosoft, made in Pretoria. Reference numbers and stuff.'

'Q-Base Holosoft sounds kind of familiar,' said Ralph.

'Oh, wait.' Luke lowered the tablet. 'That's freaky. This chip isn't just for identification. It's actually recording information. Right now.'

'About the springbok?' said Robyn. 'What sort of information?'

'I dunno. Measuring her heart rate, vital signs and stuff?' He frowned. 'It's even got a GPS tracker in it. Why would anyone care where a little springbok goes?'

'They could care a lot,' said Ralph, suddenly inspired. 'This ewe was one of a whole bunch of springbok left out as bait for the thing that got Jari and the elephant. It ate all the others. Which means a whole lot of trackers in its gut . . .'

'Which would lead whoever was after it straight back to the thing's lair,' Robyn breathed. 'So they could catch it again!'

'That's pretty smart,' said Luke.

'Gerhard's springbok is being used to track something Gerhard is after. It proves there's a link between him and the creature,' Robyn said triumphantly.

'We need to show this stuff to Dad,' said Ralph. 'Luke, can you mail me that info?'

'No worries.' Luke copied the data and put it in an email. 'Just tell your dad it's my mad skills that made it possible, yeah? Maybe he'll tell my dad and get him off my back a bit.' He frowned. 'Aw, man, I forgot to tell Rameet to get on with installing that camera here. We're three hours into overtime already, but we won't finish tomorrow if we don't stick to schedule.'

'Just do it quietly,' Robyn said, eyeing the ewe, lying wide-eyed in her pen. 'I wonder just what those chips are recording.'

'Well, I know what I'll be recording tomorrow morning,' Luke told Ralph. 'Victory over you, little brat!'

Ralph's satellite phone chimed as Luke's message came through. 'For this, maybe I'll even let you win a match,' he said. Then he followed Robyn as she hurried from the pens, heading for the examination room in the next block of outbuildings.

'Slow down,' Ralph called. But he knew Robyn was in one of her 'force of nature' moods. She swept into the block like a force nine gale; Ralph just got his toe to the double doors before they swung shut on him. He ran down the corridor and caught up with Robyn just as she pushed open the door to the observation room.

Their dad whirled around, looking surprised by the two unexpected visitors. But Ralph and Robyn stared past him, at the paper Niko was holding up to the glass partition between this room and the examination area.

Paper that bore a bloody thumbprint and words scrawled in blue biro:

GERHARD RESERVE — HIDDEN PARK
PRES. MBATO
GENETIC ENGINEERING
TROPHY HUNTING
PREDASAUR KILLING
INDAH 0818 934992

Ralph felt a chill go through him. 'What the hell does all *that* mean?'

7

Robyn sat on a soft black couch in the Lodge's living room, sipping the coffee she'd been given but barely tasting it. After she and Ralph had burst into the examination room, Roland Ballantyne had called a family council of war to discuss the day's events. The ventilating skylights in the living room's double-height vaulted timber ceiling were still open to the noisy summer night, bats and insects performing intricate ballets to the thrumming music of the cicadas.

Ralph was slumped on a beanbag on the floor. Roland passed him a glass of water.

'Where's Niko?' asked Ralph.

'It's a *family* meeting,' Robyn muttered.

Roland shot her a look. 'Niko will be joining us soon. She has something to take care of first, though.'

'That's Niko. Always caring,' said Robyn with an exaggerated pout.

Ralph broke in to change the subject. 'This day just gets crazier,' he said. 'It's like some weird nightmare.'

Robyn nodded. 'Where do we even start to go through what's happened? Viruses, giant beasts, trophy hunting, a bionic springbok. Oh, and Ralph's favourite video game, of course.'

'*PREDASAUR KILLING*, the note said,' Ralph mused. 'Maybe Gerhard found a real predasaur? I mean, whatever's been attacking the animals is acting like a predasaur – big, wild, savage, unstoppable. Perhaps Gerhard's been doing genetic experiments . . .'

'Hear that whoosh?' said Robyn. 'That's the sound of your imagination running away with you.'

'It's that mention of President Mbato and trophy hunting that's troubling me,' Roland admitted.

'Stefan was probably delirious,' said Robyn.

'Gerhard backed Mbato's campaign to be president,' Roland reminded her, 'so that Mbato would sell him a chunk of Kruger Park so he could build his reserve. It's obvious Gerhard will be pressing him to reverse the ban on trophy hunting after the upcoming elections.'

'I still can't believe Mbato got into power,' said Ralph. 'It's only because the woman from the Green Freedom Party was killed by that maniac.'

Robyn remembered the news footage all too well – presidential favourite murdered in her bed by a right-wing gun fanatic. The irony was that Mbato was voted in after vowing to crack down on such crimes, but the killer of the Green Freedom Party politician had never been found.

'Do you still reckon Mbato arranged the hit on her himself?' she asked.

'Yes,' said Roland. 'After what I went through with Mbato in the Recces, I always knew he was a dirtbag.'

Here we go, thought Ralph. The Recces was the nickname for South Africa's Special Forces Unit; Roland and Mbato had served with Xai in the regiment, almost thirty years ago. Ralph didn't know all the details, but he knew that one mission had gone badly wrong. Some men had died, and Dad and Xai blamed Mbato. All three had left the Special Forces soon after.

'We don't know that Mbato had anything to do with Gauda, though,' Ralph argued.

'Only the president could action a military strike like that,' said Roland.

'What about a private security group?' said Robyn. 'Your Special Forces mates might have heard something?'

'Perhaps,' Roland agreed. 'But we're talking black ops – covert, unofficial. Deniable. And clearly well funded.'

They all jumped when the door opened suddenly. But it was only Niko. Her face was ashen as she stood framed in the doorway.

Roland crossed to her and put an arm around her shoulders. 'Did you get through?'

Niko nodded, and Robyn suddenly realised. 'You called the number at the bottom of Stefan's note, didn't you? Indah's number.'

'Indah is Stefan's girlfriend.' Niko took the mug of coffee Roland pushed into her hands and perched on a chair. 'I suppose he just wanted someone to tell the poor woman what had happened to him.'

'Because he knew he was threatened. Even if he survived the virus, someone was coming for him,' Robyn said.

'That whole military operation – you think it was all about Stefan? He was the target?' Ralph leaned forward in his beanbag. 'What did you tell Indah?'

'She was already in shock over losing Stefan, as you can imagine. The two of them often visited his mother in Gauda. To know that everyone and everything there was gone . . .' Niko shook her head sadly and sipped her coffee. 'I said I'd seen Stefan as a patient that morning because he had some unusual symptoms, and I needed some background info on him.'

'Did you give her your –'

'Don't worry, I used a false name. And Luke showed me how to disguise my number.'

'Good,' said Roland.

'So what did Indah say?' Ralph pushed her.

'Apparently, Stefan worked for a software developer, Q-Base Holosoft.'

'No way,' Ralph breathed. 'They made the chip in the springbok.'

'Gerhard's chip,' Robyn added.

'Indah said she hadn't seen much of him this last year. He'd been away for long stretches with his work. Travelling, so he said. And get this – a few days ago she found out he'd visited the Josef Gerhard Reserve.'

'Everything leads back to Gerhard,' Roland murmured. 'Go on.'

'The Gerhard visit was meant to be secret but he let it slip when he got sick shortly after coming home. He took time off work and went to see a doctor in Pretoria, who thought he had a bad case of flu. Indah was away with her own work so Stefan went to stay at his mother's place . . .'

'Where he passed on this mystery virus, and it took down most of the village,' said Ralph.

'And then a military force swooped in,' Robyn went on.

'Trying to contain the virus,' Niko agreed. 'Though obviously I didn't tell Indah that. Better she believes the cover story.'

'A tragic accident,' Roland muttered bitterly.

'If that virus gets out, there's a whole world of tragedy to come,' said Niko. 'The viral proteins are unlike anything I've ever seen. They go nuclear on blood cells – they devastate them.'

Robyn felt her cheeks flush. Just the word 'virus' made her ache inside. 'Do you think they *have* contained it?' she said. 'If Stefan went to a doctor in Pretoria, could he have spread it before he reached Gauda?'

'We'll find out in the next twenty-four hours,' said Roland grimly.

'I should warn people,' said Niko. 'Tell them what –'

'We've been through that,' Roland said firmly. 'There's no proof left at the village. And you mustn't draw attention to yourself. If it comes out that you know what really happened in Gauda, you'll be a target for those behind it.'

'Besides, there's no proof left, is there,' said Robyn. 'Why would anyone believe us?'

'Until the deaths start mounting up,' muttered Ralph.

'On which happy note, it's time you kids went to bed,'

Roland said. 'Don't argue. You've both been through real ordeals today.'

'We're not little children, Dad!' Robyn snapped.

'Then don't act like one,' Roland retorted. 'Exhaustion clouds the mind. I need you all fresh for whatever tomorrow brings.' He smiled at her and Ralph. 'Go on. Hop it.'

Ralph and Robyn rose and walked over to the door. Robyn heard Dad say to Niko: 'Xai's in the garage, checking the cabin cruiser engines in case our mysterious trespassers come back in their amphibs. I want you to tell him all you can about that raid. Every detail. Anything that stood out – the soldiers' accents, any combat moves they made, any details about their uniform – anything that might help him ID the soldiers involved.'

Robyn glowered at her dad from the doorway. '*I* should be telling Xai that.'

'So tell him in the morning,' Ralph said. 'I'm exhausted. I bet you are too. It's not like all this crap is going to be magically gone when we open our eyes. Is it?'

The first thing Robyn saw when she woke up the next day was an enormous black-bound book on her bedside table. Dust motes swam in the morning sunbeams around it.

She recognised it in an instant: *The Adventurists*, as Ralph liked to call the journal, the personal history of the Ballantynes down the centuries, bulging with memories snatched from history's fire. Robyn sat up in bed and reached over for the enormous book. What was it doing here? Dad didn't normally like her and Ralph to go through it by themselves.

The pages inside were thick and yellowed, tattooed with lines of scratchy black scrawl. Robyn flicked through to the back of the book, where a fountain pen had been tucked inside, a sheet of modern A4 paper was fastened to the old page, and a more legible hand had written in indigo ink. The letter was dated today. It was her dad's handwriting.

Robyn,

By the time you read this, Niko and I will have left for Pretoria with Xai to check up on the doctor Stefan visited and to call on some of my old Recces to see if they know anything. I know you will be upset not to come with us, but I need you at home to keep an eye on the animals. (Yes, I am including Ralph there.)

I'm so proud of you, Robyn. Niko said that the way you carried yourself in such a dangerous situation in Gauda was remarkable. Not just a chip off the old block, but the whole potato! So I am inviting you to add your voice to our family album and write up your adventure. Just remember – choose your words with care. Who knows how many generations of Ballantyne will read them in the future?

Back tonight. Boerewors for dinner, OK?

Love wherever, whenever

Dad

Robyn stared at the page, a cold feeling building in her belly. So, Roland and Niko had dumped her safely at home while they went off chasing all the answers, leaving her to sit about and wait to see if Jari lived or died.

'Sorry, Dad,' she muttered. 'You don't get to tell me when my adventure's done.'

She put the book back on the table. She would grab a shower and check on Jari, and then . . .

And then she would see.

'Ready to meet your doom?'

Ralph's heart skipped as he turned in his chair to find Luke framed in the doorway to the den. 'Oh, wow. I didn't notice the time.'

'I'm early,' Luke said. 'Rameet said he could manage without me. In fact, he said he'd get the job done quicker. Anyway, you have an excellent space here.'

'Yeah, it's decent,' Ralph agreed modestly. The den was a large, open-plan space with exposed brickwork, dominated by a full-sized snooker table. Games consoles stood beneath a 70-inch TV screen on the wall, but there was also more old-school entertainment on offer – vintage pinball tables, car simulators and fruit machines collected by Roland over the years formed a stretch of flickering neon nostalgia along most of one wall.

'Sorry, I'm not quite with it today,' Ralph went on. 'Waiting to hear from Rob about Jari. The vet's back to change his dressings and check him over.'

'Jari will be fine. Stop making excuses for when I thrash you.' Luke grinned and hurled himself down into a beanbag. 'Go on then. Fire up the console.'

With a sigh, Ralph did as Luke said, though he really wasn't in the mood. He'd found it hard to sleep last night despite being so tired, his head whirling with all the dark events of the day. Which should he be more afraid of – a monster roaming the reserve or a deadly virus ready to kick off a pandemic? He looked at Luke, who was slumped in the beanbag, gazing around, relaxed and apparently happy. *Why can't I be more like him?* he thought.

'Hey, Ralph!' Luke sat up straight and pointed a finger at the loading screen for *Predasaur*. 'Check the credits.'

Ralph glanced over and froze. 'Motion capture by Q-Base Holosoft,' he read aloud. 'I knew I'd heard the name! The same people who made the chip inside the springbok make *Predasaur*!'

'How freaky is that?' said Luke.

'Totally.' Ralph stared at the screen. 'It means Gerhard is linked to the making of this game.'

'Motion capture,' said Luke thoughtfully. 'That's when they film something, turn it digital and then map computer graphics on top of it, right?'

'Maybe the springbok chip is recording how it moves and stuff,' Ralph suggested. 'So they can use it later.'

'Maybe they use a real sarcosuchus too,' Luke joked. 'Just picked one up from, like, a zillion years ago and brought it back to make it a star.'

'Genetic engineering,' Ralph breathed. He thought of the note Niko and Robyn had brought back from Gauda: Niko's patient, Stefan, had worked for Q-Base Holosoft too. There had to be a link. 'I told Dad and Rob yesterday that Gerhard could be trying to make his own predasaurs . . .'

'So he doesn't just help create *Predasaur*, he breeds the bosses too? Get a grip, you conspiracy nerd,' Luke told him with a smirk. 'And get a controller. I'm in a hurry to whup your ass.'

But Ralph was already running out of the room.

He ran into Robyn coming the other way, from the direction of the recovery pens. She had placed the springbok in a harness and was leading her across the courtyard.

'Rob, I was just coming to find you,' he said. 'What's she doing out?'

'She's better,' Robyn said. 'Needs exercise.'

'Right.' Ralph nodded. 'Well, get this: the company Stefan worked for – the same company that made the chip you're taking for a walk, well – guess what?'

Robyn didn't look interested. 'Jari's got worse,' she informed her brother. 'The vet says he could die. The next twenty-four hours are critical.'

Ralph bit his lip. 'I'm sorry. I was going to ask, but . . .'

'But you're more concerned about the chip,' Robyn said coldly.

'It's just that Gerhard's involved with *Predasaur*, somehow. Q-Base Holosoft helped to make the game as well as that chip in the springbok,' Ralph said. 'The creature that hurt Jari . . . the springbok it attacked . . . the guy who got the virus, who visited Gerhard's reserve and then wiped out Gauda – that software company links everything somehow.'

'Links it to Gerhard,' Robyn agreed, as the springbok

strained on her leash as if in fear of the name. 'And maybe through him to Mbato. To the *president*.'

'It's huge,' said Ralph. 'If Dad can find out something from his old army mates, maybe he and Niko can start building a case against them.'

'Maybe they're not the only ones,' Robyn said quietly. 'Look, Ralph, I'll go crazy if I have to sit here all day waiting to hear about Jari. I need to do something.'

Ralph gave her a suspicious look. 'Like what?'

'Aren't you meant to be playing Luke soon?'

'Yeah, but I'm not really feeling it.'

'Good,' said Robyn. 'Because I've got something better in mind for all of us.'

8

'Off-road trip!' Luke cried, yanking on the wheel and steering the Crocodile Lodge jeep off the path.

Ralph, sitting in the back, banged his head as the vehicle bounced over the rough ground. 'Watch it!' he yelled. 'I thought you'd actually passed your test?'

'When you're old enough to drive, I'll listen to your lectures.'

'Careful, Luke!' Robyn told him, as the springbok shifted in her holding case. 'Sick animal back here.'

'That's no way to talk about your brother, Rob! Still, maybe you're right.' Luke slowed down and steered more carefully around a huge tree stump.

Ralph sat back and sighed. The dart gun felt cold and hard against his hip in its holster. 'Do you think we're doing the right thing?'

'Don't start this again.' Robyn turned around from the front seat and glared at him. 'I love the springbok, but we need it off our property. Luke says it's transmitting something – we don't know what. Gerhard could be using it to spy on us for all we know.'

'It could be, like, the Trojan Springbok,' Luke put in. 'You've taken it into the heart of your camp and now Gerhard's inside with it. Watching you.'

'All right,' Ralph muttered, creeped out despite himself. 'I'm surprised, though, Rob. I mean, that springbok could be evidence or something.'

'If anything, Gerhard could twist it into evidence that we're holding on to stolen property!' Robyn retorted. 'Anyway, what are we going to do – cut the poor ewe open and pull out the chip?'

'The question's more like, what are we going to do if Luke can't get through Gerhard's security and open the gate onto his reserve?' Ralph said.

'I got you the dirt on the chip, didn't I?' Luke said. 'Seriously, I'm good at using the tech we make. I just suck at the installation, the admin, the time-keeping . . .'

'So you're basically saying you'd be a better burglar than a worker,' Robyn summed up.

'Pretty much,' Luke agreed.

The morning was warming up, and all around were the calls, croaks and chirrups of the wildlife. Mopane trees formed a dense thicket in the forested area ahead of them, their butterfly-shaped leaves barely moving in the hot breeze that drifted through the reserve. The breeze brought with it the scent of wild sage and the sharp aroma of giant turpentine grass. They were soon entering a ravine, a gentle slope bordered by stone walls. Jackalberry trees grew more thickly here and the canopy soon closed over them, hiding the jeep as it purred along, each bump in the path bringing them closer to Gerhard's estate.

'We're nearly there,' said Robyn as the path sloped down towards a wall of stout baobab trees with a giant pile of boulders off to the right. 'And through there is our gateway to Gerhard's territory.'

When Luke had parked the jeep, Robyn struggled to put on a heavy-looking rucksack.

'Going on holiday?' Ralph joked.

'Being prepared,' said Robyn. She took the springbok out of the transport case and attached a lead to her harness. Ralph felt a rush of nerves as he stepped out into the heat. Then he pushed his doubts away. His dad, his grandfather and his ancestors before him – they had all defied expectation, chancing their luck, acting on instinct.

Taking risks was his birthright.

Ralph led the way through the narrow gap in the rocks. Listening intently for possible threats, but hearing none, he beckoned Robyn and Luke through after him. The springbok trotted at Robyn's side as if she was the herd mother or something.

They walked on for another ten minutes, until they saw the looming black solid perimeter fence dividing the land. As they got closer, the hum of electricity in the fence made Ralph's teeth hurt, and he retreated behind a nearby tree. Robyn and Luke joined him as they tried to suss out the set-up. A metal gate had been built into the barrier, big enough for a truck to pass through. There was an entry coder and intercom attached to the gate's opening mechanism, and a camera pointing down.

'This security looks like the real deal,' said Robyn warily.

'Sure, the fence has anti-intruder defences, but we've got a key,' said Luke.

'We have?'

'Right there. Your springbok.'

Ralph looked at him. 'Meaning?'

'That chip inside it,' Luke explained. 'Gerhard wouldn't want an alarm sounding every time his animals wandered too close to the fence, right? So that clever transmitting chip disarms the system when chipped animals come close to it.'

'But it won't open the gate,' Ralph pointed out. 'Or all the animals would be in and out of there the whole time.'

'Yes, but the chip talks to Gerhard's security system, and that interaction gives us a sneaky way into the perimeter security codes.' Luke went on. 'Remember that chip was a fifth-generation clone? Well, I can clone it too and download a copy to your phones. It'll be like we've *all* been chipped.'

'When we come out here, we take Croc Lodge handsets like all the other rangers,' said Robyn, showing Luke the sleek phone with its branded lock screen. 'They're satellite based – easier to trace when we're working all over the reserve.'

Ralph nodded and pulled out his own phone. 'Will your software work on them?'

'I guess we'll see.' Luke got busy scanning the springbok's chip and converting the data into something the phones' operating system could use. Then he bluetoothed it over to Ralph and Robyn. Warily, Ralph started forward. But, with sudden courage, Robyn marched past him and hovered just out of range of the security camera.

She pulled nervously at the straps of her rucksack. 'But how do we open this gate and get past the camera and go *in*?'

'Chill. VanRok has designed a tonne of software to get around this kind of thing. Usually for counter-terrorist operations – you know, so Special Forces can gain quick access to enemy strongholds, stuff like that.' Luke grinned amiably. 'I've got software that can mess with a security system's clock. It thinks two nanoseconds have gone by – in fact, it's two *minutes*. Then the software resets the clock and wipes itself from the system.'

'Clever,' Ralph admitted.

'Best of all, it's pretty much point-and-shoot.' Luke pointed his phone at the entry coder. With a bone-jarring rattle, the gate slid open.

Ralph stared at the gap in the fence, and the bushland beyond. He held his breath, waiting for the din of a siren. But all was peaceful.

'Whoa,' said Ralph. 'That's crazy. You did it, Luke!'

'Nice work,' said Robyn. 'I'm impressed.'

'What can I say? It's the family business.' Luke smiled but looked apprehensive. 'So, here you go. Let the springbok of doom through the gate and we can get back to Croc Lodge.'

Robyn shifted the rucksack on her shoulders and took a deep breath. 'I'm not going back yet.'

Ralph stared at her. 'What?'

'We've got an open door to Gerhard's territory!' Robyn said. 'What happened to the elephant, the croc, and to Jari – it's got to be linked to his reserve.'

'Look, Rob,' said Luke, 'I get you're upset about your pet lion, but –'

'Of course I'm upset!' she hissed. 'If we could find evidence – film it and show it to people . . .'

'Evidence of a giant deadly predator! Nice.' Ralph shook his head. 'Oh, and don't forget the new killer virus Stefan might've picked up from a visit here. We could maybe take away a deadly infection as evidence, too.'

'Whoa, what?' Luke looked appalled.

'We're outdoors – *way* outdoors – and the whole point is that we won't come close to anyone,' Robyn said. 'This is just a scouting mission. But if we do find something that looks bad, think of the damage it could do Gerhard!'

'Luke's right,' said Ralph. 'This is a revenge thing for Jari.'

'For so many animals,' Robyn said. 'You heard Dad: Mbato and Gerhard are great mates. Trophy hunting *will* come back unless we can do something to discredit them.'

'So now you're taking on the president as well as Gerhard and a killer virus?' Luke spluttered. 'I didn't sign up for this.'

'Please, Luke,' Robyn urged him. 'We need you.'

'Who's "we"?' said Ralph. 'This is crazy. I've got one tranquilliser gun, no supplies, and you expect me to just walk in there?' Then he clocked the bulky rucksack she wore and groaned softly. 'Water? Food? More tranq guns and darts?'

'All of the above,' Robyn confirmed. 'Come on, Ralph. This is our chance to show Dad he doesn't need to treat us like helpless little kids.' She looked at Luke. 'And it's your chance to show people what you can do. You could let it be known that you're the guy who broke through Josef Gerhard's security.'

Luke considered. 'I guess if he finds out I could be, like, *Yeah, that was me. You need me, man, I've got skill*s. I could even *tell* him it was me.'

Ralph saw the conflict on Robyn's face; she was clearly revolted by the idea of Luke wanting to work for Gerhard, but didn't want to discourage him if he was coming around to the idea. 'Sure,' she said at last.

'Of course, if Gerhard catches us, you won't need to tell him,' Ralph said. 'You can just spill it to the cops.'

'If Gerhard does catch us, it'll be fine. Cos we have the perfect excuse.' Robyn shrugged innocently. 'We're just being helpful kids, taking his lost property back to him.'

'The springbok!' Ralph half-smiled. 'Got it all figured out, haven't you?'

'Pretty much,' said Robyn, smiling back. 'Imagine if we find evidence that shows Gerhard is up to really bad stuff. It'll liven up your chapter in *The Adventurists*, won't it?'

'I guess . . .' Ralph nodded. 'OK. I'm game.'

'Game? Bad choice of words, bruh.' Luke shook his head. 'On Gerhard's land, I'm guessing the game doesn't last long.'

'We're running out of time,' said Robyn. 'I'm going in.' She strode through the gate, the springbok trotting along after her. Ralph sighed. Returning the springbok *was* a pretty good excuse for their being there – if you overlooked the breaking and entering.

'I'd better keep an eye on her.' He looked at Luke. 'You in?'

Luke shrugged and pushed out a sigh. 'I guess it beats working for a living, right?'

'Come on, then,' Ralph said, and followed his sister. 'Let's make for cover before we're seen.'

The gate slid shut behind them with a squeal. The rattle as the bolt slid home was almost like an iron chuckle.

'Guess there's no turning back now, huh?' Luke said.

Robyn wiped the sweat from her forehead as she walked along with the springbok, Luke and Ralph close behind. They'd been here for some time now. The sun had climbed as high as it would and was making tracks towards the west as they headed deeper into Gerhard territory. But she knew they would have to turn around at some point. She hoped they could get out as easily as they got in.

Time's still on our side, she reflected. She imagined that Roland, Xai and Niko would spend the whole day in Pretoria, and it was more than a three-hour drive to get there. But if Dad got back to the Lodge first, they would find Ralph and Robyn gone and no note left to say where they were. What would he do then?

Being an Adventurist isn't as easy as it sounds, thought Robyn.

On they went through the savannah, tranq guns in their hands – even Luke, once Ralph had trained him in how to use it. Not that there was evidence of much big game around the place. *Gerhard's probably had it all shot,* Robyn thought darkly. *I bet he has a hundred stuffed heads mounted on his wall.*

She welcomed the heart-lifting sight of herds of oribi – graceful little dwarf antelopes – and a giraffe with its young, browsing the leaves of thorn trees.

'Isn't it time we let the springbok go and got out of here ourselves?' Luke grumbled. 'We haven't found anything, and I'm starving.'

'Soon.' Robyn handed him the bag of Brazil nuts she'd brought. 'We've gone through so much to get here, we can't just leave.'

'Maybe we should.' Ralph's voice floated down to them. He was halfway up a moss-covered yellowwood, looking through his binoculars. 'There's another fence ahead. Can't see any rangers, but it's got to be five metres high, with barbed wire along the top.'

'If Gerhard has something to hide,' said Robyn, 'it'll be behind that fence.'

'Great,' said Luke. 'Well, let's come back another day and work out the best way in.'

Robyn gave him a sharp look. 'Give up, you mean?'

Ralph dropped down from the branch. 'How about we skirt the perimeter with our friendly springbok and try to find a way in? Luke will think of something.'

'No pressure, then,' Luke grumbled.

Once they'd got past the yellowwood trees it didn't take them long to reach the fence. They walked along it for a good five hundred metres, sticking to the cover of the trees where they could, until they reached a solid gate built into the barrier. No one was about; the electric hum of the inner fence sang for their ears alone. Ralph approached with the springbok, but this time the hum did not fade. Instead, it became sharp and high pitched, making the ewe shift restlessly. Suddenly she strained to get away and nearly

87

pulled him over. The ewe broke his grip and raced away into the bushes.

'Wait!' Robyn called, but the springbok was long gone, the lead trailing behind it. 'Poor thing. Running might make her injury worse. I hope she's OK.'

'I hope *we* are.' Luke pulled out his phone and studied the screen. 'Security for this fence has been taken up *several* notches. This fence stays electric. If an animal gets close, its tag triggers a high-frequency sonic bombardment to scare it away.'

Robyn rubbed her forehead. 'Which means the electric part of the fence . . .'

'Is for intruders, like us,' Ralph finished. 'For anyone who managed to get past the outer fence.'

'If you touch this one, it's strong enough to knock you down,' Luke reported. 'Maybe even kill you.'

A chill sweat trickled down Robyn's back. 'Which means that Gerhard has stuff going on in there he's ready to kill people to protect.'

Ralph nodded. 'But what?'

9

Ralph eyed the gate in Gerhard's security fence: the final barrier to whatever lay beyond. Beside him, Luke fiddled with the settings on his security app, trying to get them through. At least, he *said* he was trying. Robyn was quietly urging him along, persuading him that things would be fine.

Would they, though? Ralph knew they were taking an insane risk, breaking and entering Gerhard's private property. But it was precisely for that reason he didn't want to back down. Robyn was right: somewhere ahead among the towering baobab and lush buffalo thorn trees there must be proof of whatever scheme Gerhard was pursuing, and if they could find evidence and expose him, then they'd be making the world a better place for people *and* animals.

'OK, I'm gonna try something,' Luke announced, breaking into Ralph's thoughts. 'One springbok sets off the sonic alarm if it comes too close to the electric fence, right? If it isn't scared away, it gets a shock big enough to hurt it badly. Even kill it.'

Ralph nodded. 'So?'

'It *is* scared away,' said Robyn. 'We saw that.'

'But what if a big herd of springbok come too close and refuse to run? Gerhard's not going to want them all dead.' Luke tapped the screen. 'I found a secondary command protocol hidden behind the sonic alarm, but I can't get a clear reading. It might be a failsafe command to shut down the electric fence so the herd isn't hurt.'

'*Might* be,' Ralph said heavily.

'But if the fence is made safe, we can climb it,' Robyn said.

'Maybe,' Ralph agreed. 'But in case you hadn't noticed, we don't have a herd of springbok handy.'

'Only we do,' said Luke, waving the phone. 'I cloned the springbok's data chip. I can copy and paste it over and over, make a virtual herd of springbok. *Trick* the sensors.'

'That's a brilliant idea.' Robyn looked genuinely impressed.

Luke grinned at her. 'Cover your ears.' He put the phone down in the grass close to the gate, tapped the screen and scuttled away.

Ralph winced as the noise pierced his head. It rose in pitch and volume, an awful vibration drilling into his skull. 'It's worse than before!' he shouted.

Robyn was bent double, her eyes tightly shut, hands clamped over her ears. 'Make it stop!'

Luke was too busy rolling on his back in pain to do anything. Ralph took a few steps towards the phone but stopped, thinking he was going to throw up. Black spots swarmed his vision. Gritting his teeth, he threw himself forward into the long grass.

Then the alarm cut out as suddenly as it had begun, and in the ringing silence that followed the gate slid slowly open.

Robyn shook her head. 'What happened? I thought you said it would just shut off the electric fence.'

'Looks like it worked even better than I thought!' Luke pushed himself up to his elbows. 'The system must be designed to open the gate and let the animals in before they hurt themselves.'

'It won't stay open for long then,' said Ralph.

Robyn helped Ralph up, picked up Luke's phone, and they staggered over to join Luke in the inner reserve. On the other side of the gate was a clear area of dry ground with scattered clumps of knee-high caterpillar grasses, the thin bobbled stalks of their flowers curling in the breeze. About fifty metres away the grassland merged into a bushveld of small shrubs and trees that were spaced widely enough that they didn't form a closed canopy layer. Ralph knew that they had to get to thicker woodland quickly, to give them more cover from animals and rangers.

'Come on,' he said. 'Let's get to that wooded area ahead of us as quickly as we can.'

'Agreed.' Robyn led the way at a brisk jog, despite the heat of the day.

Ralph was pleased to see signs of recent grazing. In their own reserve, he and Robyn helped keep an eye on the balance of grasslands and treed areas to provide the best environment for both prey and hunting animals, and they would occasionally move herds to new locations to keep the vegetation under control. Whatever else Gerhard was up to, his rangers looked to be doing a decent job of managing the environment.

They kept to cover as much as possible, tranq guns in their hands, dashing through clumps of jackalberry trees and shrubby bushwillows, watching carefully for signs of hunters or prey. Ralph argued that finding a hunting party would give them clues as to where Gerhard's high-value animals were; then maybe they could grab the evidence they sought. But all the time, he couldn't help thinking: *How will we get back out?*

It wasn't long before Ralph heard the clear, high repeated call of a fish eagle from somewhere ahead of them. 'The river's in that direction. Best chance of seeing a hunt in action.'

Robyn nodded and they angled through the trees towards the sound.

After thirty sweat-soaked minutes, they came to an outcrop overlooking the river – the same river that ran through their land.

Ralph holstered his gun and hid in a clump of tall finger grass. Robyn did the same and pulled a pair of binoculars from her rucksack as a herd of mid-sized antelope edged into sight, heading cautiously for the water.

'More springbok,' Luke surmised, shifting in the grass beside them.

'No. They're impala,' Robyn told him. 'Impala are more active throughout the day, springbok come out at dawn or dusk.'

'Nature. I love it,' said Luke. 'So, why are we watching them?'

'This is our best chance to get some evidence,' said Robyn.

'If hunters are out today, they'll likely follow the herd, cos the herd draws out predators like the big cats. And that's what the hunters are gunning for.'

The impala were still making slowly for the river; it was deep and fast, but with some more shallower parts. The bank was made of red earth with rocky outcrops, with patches of long grasses.

'Jeez, just drink the water already,' Luke muttered. 'What are those things scared of?'

'Plenty,' said Ralph. 'They're prey for just about everything with teeth.'

Robyn looked through the binoculars and nodded. 'See the little cluster of taller trees ahead of us? Look high: there's a leopard, staying out of sight.'

'The leopard will pounce sooner or later and bring down an impala,' said Ralph. 'While it's occupied, the hunters will most likely kill the leopard and then maybe come for a trophy shot. If they do, we'll get video proof of illegal activity on Gerhard's land.'

'And they'll never even know we're watching.' Robyn smiled. 'Today, the trophy hunters are *our* prey.'

'I can hear something,' Ralph said. 'A motor. Coming from downriver.' He crawled across to Robyn, reaching for the binoculars. She passed them over.

Sure enough, Ralph saw two amphibious boats coming into view around a curve of the river. Each had eight huge tyres, lifting the body of the boats above the surface of the river. About half a dozen armed men were in the open cabin of each boat. At the prow of the second craft stood a large man. His face was shielded by the brim of his hat, but his jacket stole all attention anyway: the front was embroidered ostentatiously with a stylised African crowned eagle – the mightiest of the hunting birds.

'D'you think those uniformed heavies are the same guys that our rangers saw?' Robyn asked him.

'Could be.' Ralph kept the binoculars trained on the boats. 'Half of those men are wearing Gerhard's ranger uniforms. And they're all carrying rifles.'

'They've got drones with them too,' whispered Luke.

'Drones?' Ralph looked back towards the amphibs and saw four of the metal surveyors drifting lazily above the boats. 'Why?'

'Filming them in action, I bet,' said Robyn. 'Nice souvenir.'

One of the drones moved ahead of the boats and hovered above the impala herd, high enough that they didn't spook.

'The leopard's getting ready to pounce,' Luke said. 'Guys, this must be the trophy. Those hunters are after the big cat.'

'I'm not so sure,' Ralph said, his eyes fixed on the man in the jacket. 'That big dude is packing a Holland Royal Double. It's like the Rolls-Royce of shotguns, kills anything that walks. Fires thousand-grain bullets the size of a chapstick at two thousand feet per second.'

Robyn shuddered. 'That's mad overkill for a leopard.'

'Emphasis on the kill,' Ralph agreed. 'And the recoil on those things is enough to dislocate your shoulder. You might use it for a charging bull elephant coming straight for you, or a buffalo about to run you down, but a leopard . . .'

'The guy's taking no chances, is all,' Luke suggested. He

trailed off as there was a sudden panic among the impalas, followed by a flash of movement as the leopard pounced out of nowhere. It had sneaked up unseen, crouching low in the long grass, then ambushed an impala before it could react. The leopard bit down on the impala's neck and twisted, breaking its bones instantly.

Robyn had her phone out and was videoing the scene. Ralph knew they needed the evidence, but he couldn't help wishing that the hunters would miss. He didn't want to see such a magnificent creature taken down. But while Jacket Man took aim, he didn't fire.

'Why's he taking his time?' Luke muttered. 'Shoot it, dude, and let's all go home.'

The rest of the impala herd had vanished. The leopard started to drag its kill towards the trees.

'What's it doing now?' said Luke.

'They like to eat in peace and quiet,' Robyn whispered, but that peace and quiet was torn apart in a heartbeat as a surge of movement erupted from the riverbank. The leopard never reached the tree. A vast animal thrust forward with horrible speed, crushing both leopard and impala in its hefty jaws. It was nearly three times the size of the largest crocodile Robyn had ever seen, with a long bulbous snout and teeth like ivory bunting – bunting stained red as it tore through the leopard, swallowing head and shoulders in a single bite.

Luke recoiled and turned away, retching.

'I don't believe it.' Robyn was still recording but was no longer looking at the screen, pale and in shock as she took in the flesh-eating frenzy on the bank. 'That's no croc. It's more like a dinosaur.'

Ralph swallowed hard, transfixed. The beast's speed and sheer ferocious power were hideous to behold. 'I think it really is a sarcosuchus. Just like you said, Luke.'

'Aw, c'mon,' said Luke. 'I was kidding.'

Robyn grabbed the binoculars back and took a closer look. 'From *Predasaur*?' She swore under her breath. 'Freaky. It looks just like it does in the game.'

'Remember Stefan's note?' Ralph said. '*Predasaur killing*. Either he meant predasaurs are killing things, like our elephant or the leopard . . . or else that hunters are hunting down predasaurs as the ultimate trophy kills.'

'Either way, that thing didn't crawl out of a video game. It's real.' Robyn tailed off, ashen-faced, as realisation struck. 'Genetic engineering. Jeez, Ralph, you were right. Gerhard's made an animal that's just *like* a predasaur.'

'The grandfather of all crocs on Earth.' Ralph couldn't drag his eyes from the monster, which was finishing its warm-blooded meal. 'And it's not walked on this planet for a hundred million years.'

10

Robyn started as gunfire broke the grisly silence. Apparently satisfied that the super-croc was oblivious to all but its meal, Jacket Man took the shot. The monster jerked with the impact. The bullet struck its scaly grey shoulder and gore sprayed out. The predasaur barked with pain, turned heavily and scuttled back towards the water with surprising speed. Another shot rang out, but sent only dust showering from the ground just beside it.

'Jacket Man missed his anchoring shot,' Ralph said.

'Anchoring shot?' Luke said, looking pale and clammy.

'Crocodile hunters aim to hit the brain or the spine with their first shot,' Robyn explained. 'Kill it straight away, or at least immobilise it, so it can't retreat to the water.'

'Like this one,' Ralph added. 'I wonder how badly it was hurt.'

The answer came in frantic yells as a terrific eruption from the water rocked and lifted one of the amphibious craft. Robyn gasped – the wounded super-croc must have risen up beneath it. One of the men on board was thrown into the water. He thrashed about for a few seconds until a huge tail swept up and slammed down on top of him. The other men on board yelled and clung on as the craft was sent spiralling across the water. From the rear boat, Jacket Man fired again into the water. The man's body floated into sight. There was a gunshot wound on his back.

Then the body was snatched back down beneath the water.

Robyn stopped recording and dropped the phone, sickened. The men on both boats started firing wildly into the crimson water, which frothed under the onslaught.

Then an awful silence fell, like smoke over a battlefield. Then came more shouting and the amphibs rolled up onto the riverbank. Jacket Man was yelling at some of the heavies and the rest stood guard with guns pointed at the water, or cast big, heavy metal hooks on long ropes into the river, pulling them back and casting them out again.

Luke's breath came in shallow gasps. 'So now they're fishing?'

'They're trying to hook the sarcosuchus and pull it out of the river,' said Ralph, grabbing Robyn's phone to keep recording. He knew that if the beast had taken enough bullets to kill it, the hunters wouldn't throw away their chance of the trophy shot. If he could only catch that moment on camera! He zoomed in for a close-up.

Then the 'recording' icon flashed and went out. *Memory Full* read the message on screen.

'No!' Ralph stabbed at the screen. 'No way! You can't be out of memory!'

'Um, the chip-cloned software is kind of memory intensive,' Luke confessed.

'We'll use mine,' Ralph said, reaching for his own phone.

'We've got enough footage,' Robyn argued. 'We should back it up to the cloud.'

Ralph nodded and tried to upload the video, but it wouldn't even begin the operation. 'There's no signal here. I don't understand. Outside the fence it was strong enough.'

'Gerhard must have some kind of suppressor here,' Luke said. 'You can use satellites to block other internet providers. He'll only have his private network working.'

'Of course,' Ralph breathed, pushing his phone back into his pocket. It made sense: if Gerhard was breeding monsters here, he would want total security. 'Well, can you connect us to his network? We have to back this up.'

'Jeez, bruh, this stuff's not magic! You know what security Gerhard's got going on – I could try for hours and get no –' Luke broke off with a strangled shout and flipped over backwards, rolling clear of the cover of the long grass. 'Something stung me!' he yelled, clutching his forearm. 'Ugh! Velvet ant!'

'Quiet!' hissed Robyn. 'They'll hear us!'

But it was too late. The men on the riverbank were pointing and shouting. One of the drones was already heading towards them.

'Oh no.' Ralph groaned and scrambled up. He gave the phone with its precious footage back to Robyn and shoved his own phone back into his pocket.

'Time to go!' Robyn snapped, stuffing the binoculars into her rucksack and scrambling to her feet. 'And hide your face – that drone's got cameras.'

Luke groaned in pain as he joined them running towards the trees. 'My arm feels like I dunked it in a deep-fat fryer.'

'If they catch us, you'll be feeling worse!' Robyn led the way into the cover of the trees. But her heart was sinking; no way would the gate they'd come in still be open. Visceral snapshots of the horrific events by the riverbank flashed through her mind and she pushed herself faster, as if hoping to outrun them.

You'll be next, her fear whispered.

Heart banging, breath burning in her throat, Robyn ran on through the scattered trees. Ralph drew level and automatically she increased her pace. Luke kept up, his arm as red and angry as his sweating face.

She glimpsed a drone following them. Sending video to the guards, no doubt, telling them exactly where their intruders were headed.

The realisation struck her like a punch to the stomach. *There's no way we're gonna get out of here.* Gerhard's land would be teeming with well-trained, well-rested guards on high alert. *Just keep running*, Robyn told herself.

With fresh determination she pushed herself harder, making for an area where the treetops touched to form a canopy that would shield them from aerial view. They reached the cover and dropped to the ground, panting for breath.

Luke looked from Ralph to Robyn. 'What now?'

Ralph drew his tranquilliser gun and peered through the trees. 'The cover looks a bit patchier to the west. I'll run that way and make sure the drone sees me. With luck it'll think we're all headed that way – but if you and Luke stick to the covered ground you should come out not far from that security gate.'

'And what then? You double back and join us?' Robyn nodded thoughtfully. 'Yeah, that might work.'

'I'll try to get that gate open again,' said Luke.

Ralph nodded. 'I'll join you as quick as I can.'

'Be careful,' Robyn hissed.

'Duh,' said Ralph, then turned and hared away through the woodland.

Robyn watched him go with a feeling of dread, then she checked the signal strength on the phone again. Still nothing. There was no way to upload the incriminating video or call for help. 'Come on,' she told Luke.

They moved as quickly and quietly as they could until they reached a thicket at the edge of open ground – with a clear view of the security gate. It was closed.

'See if you can do that time-stretching trick again,' Robyn suggested.

Luke fiddled with the security app and waited. 'No good.'

'What?'

'It's giving us nothing.' Luke tapped frantically at the phone. 'I can't get into the system. They must have locked it down since we triggered the alarm.' He shook his head and glared at her. 'I said we should go. But you had to stay on, had to get your precious evidence . . .'

'All right, I'm sorry, I'm sorry.' Robyn stared longingly at the unmoving gate. 'Come on, Luke, try again.'

And then she heard the roar.

It was like a scream of rage wrenched from the ancient land, its echo lost in the crunch and rustle of broken undergrowth. Something huge was running towards them.

Luke stared, horror-struck, at Robyn. 'What the hell?'

She shook her head. She recognised the creature's footfalls after spending so much time with Jari and Sabal – only this tread was cranked up to eleven. 'It's a big cat.' She pulled Luke back towards a tree, already gauging how quickly she could climb it. 'A *really* big cat.'

'Move!' Ralph burst from some nearby bushes, his face red with exertion and etched with terror. His own footsteps had been lost in the rampage of whatever was coming. 'We can't hide. Can't climb. We have to *run*.'

'Wait,' Luke said. 'Your dart gun!'

'Drone knocked it out of my hand!' Ralph hurtled past them, breaking the cover of the treeline. 'Seriously, *run*!' Robyn shoved Luke after Ralph and ran too, making for the gate and the sentry box beside it.

Another roar sent birds wheeling from the trees. Robyn glanced over her shoulder and for a moment she froze in deep, primeval terror.

A lion stood at the treeline, but a lion unlike any she had ever seen before. It was over two metres long and stood almost as tall as a human. Its muscles bunched and twitched under its grey, shaggy fur. Each paw was as big as her face. The lion's head was ringed by a ragged, bloodstained mane and its teeth were bared. Strings of drool hung from its teeth. Its eyes were a bright, shocking red, as if the blood vessels had burst. *What could cause that?* Robyn wondered.

Then the moment was broken by the *phut-phut* of tranquilliser darts. One passed through the lion's mane, the other caught it in the neck. The lion roared again, anger mixed with a terrible, all-consuming pain as it staggered backwards. Jolted into action, Robyn fired her own two darts into its chest – and instantly felt guilty as hell. One dart was enough to take down a buffalo; three would surely kill this beast. The lion roared angrily and fell back on its haunches.

'That thing's from *Predasaur* too,' Luke hissed. 'End-of-level boss, it's killed me thirty times.'

Incredibly, with a brutal snarl, the lion got up, despite the darts, and shook its gigantic head as if to clear it. It took a stumbling step towards them.

'No way,' Luke breathed. 'Why won't it stay down?'

'Too powerful,' Robyn whispered.

'Come on!' Ralph yelled from the gates. Robyn's every instinct screamed at her to run, but instead she forced herself to keep eye contact with the creature. To reach out to it, like she had with Jari and Sabal when they were cubs. To try to connect.

But it was no use. Robyn couldn't read the lion's reactions, couldn't shake the feeling that there was more than just space between them. There was *time*. This lion, in all his brutal splendour, looked more primitive than others she had seen. He didn't belong here – and she sensed, somehow, that he knew it. She backed away slowly, calmly, her eyes locked on the lion's, still trying to connect.

But the lion roared again and bounded towards her.

11

Robyn knew she was dead. She watched death run towards her, pounding over the ground, its sharp teeth beckoning to her bones. As she backed away, she stumbled and fell.

Suddenly, blue electric crackles swarmed over the lion, stopping it in its tracks. It roared in defiance, but a further blast of electricity shook it harder and the beast rolled over onto its side, twitching.

Robyn stared, numb, unable to believe she'd been saved. The lion had been zapped with a Taser. She looked up and found two of Gerhard's park wardens standing over her.

A bearded man glared down at her. 'Are you all right?' he asked.

'I . . . I think so,' Robyn said.

'Good,' said a hard-faced woman with a blond buzz cut and dark eyes. 'That means I can do this.' She kicked Robyn in the ribs, her steel toecaps striking bone. Robyn cried out and rolled over, winded.

'Leave her alone!' Ralph shouted from somewhere nearby.

'Best not, Abi,' Beardy told the woman. 'Leave something for Shrinker, yeah?'

Shrinker. Robyn remembered her dad mentioning him: Gerhard's security chief. She stayed hunched over, rubbing her throbbing ribs, partly because they hurt like hell but also to buy time to think.

But time was up already. The woman hauled Robyn to her feet and frisked her thoroughly, with Beardy standing by, Taser in hand.

Maybe she could play dumb, pretend to be a tourist excited about seeing big game. Would harmless curiosity fly with the guards?

'Look, we're sorry, OK?' she said, acting close to tears. 'We heard you had amazing animals here and we just wanted to see them. We didn't mean any harm.'

'The little-girl-lost act might have worked better if you people hadn't used pro-grade hackware on the security system,' said Beardy, leaning over her.

Luke cursed at the guards trying to hold him, and they ordered him to settle down. She heard yelling, and twisted around to see that Luke had managed to break free and was running for the gate. The guard who was frisking Ralph broke off to help recapture Luke. Soon, a group of them had Tasers held to Luke's chest. Finally, he stopped struggling.

'Hold still,' said the hard-faced woman, checking the pockets of Robyn's trousers.

Beardy reached over and grabbed her phone, which was peeping out from the top of her shirt pocket. 'I'll be taking this too, thanks.'

'No!' Robyn gasped. 'Give it back.'

'Oh! OK then. Here.' Beardy held it out to her, then

snatched it away when she reached for it. 'Sorry, Miss Ballantyne. Too slow.' He smirked and put it in his own pocket.

'What?' Robyn tried not to blush as she glared at Beardy. 'Who's Miss Ballantyne?'

'Do you want another kick in the ribs?' Abi smiled unpleasantly. 'Robyn Alice Ballantyne?'

Robyn swapped a helpless look with Ralph. *So much for bluffing. She knows too much about us already.*

'Look at you,' Abi jeered. 'Trying so hard to act in control when you're so afraid. I can take someone like you and break them like I'd snap a twig.' She snorted and turned to the other wardens. 'Get them all in the jeep.'

Beardy yanked Robyn to her feet. 'Come on.'

Luke and Ralph were shoved into the back of the jeep, a warden on either side of them. Robyn was forced into the passenger seat while Abi took the wheel. Beardy got into another vehicle and rolled off ahead of them.

'Look, we were just bringing back one of Mr Gerhard's springbok,' said Ralph. 'It got on our land.'

Luke nodded. 'And we were gonna ring the doorbell or whatever, but the ID chip in the springbok just opened the gate.'

'Gee, I'm sure it totally did, Luke and Ralph!' said Abi sarcastically. 'Just like that.'

'It's true. Check your database.' Robyn glared at Abi. 'You'll see how it *mysteriously* got across into our property.'

'Prey animals run.' Abi glanced at her, eyes cold and dark. 'But they don't always run the right way. Do they, Robyn?'

'Speaking of the wrong way,' said Ralph quickly, 'you're taking us away from the gate. Aren't you going to escort us off your land?'

'When you went to so much trouble to get here? Nuh-uh. Mr Gerhard's Head of Security is so keen to meet you.'

'Shrinker,' said Robyn with a shiver of fear.

'Wait,' Ralph said suddenly, staring out at the landscape. 'What are *they*?'

Luke swore. 'I don't believe it.'

'Why so surprised?' mocked Abi. 'You'd heard of the amazing animals here, remember?'

Robyn followed the boys' line of sight and gasped.

A herd of rhinos was grazing in the savannah. But these weren't ordinary rhinos. They had two horns: a large one that jutted forward and a smaller one between their dark red eyes. They had a layer of coarse hair on their backs and shorter hair on their bodies and legs. They had stocky legs and a large hump on their shoulders. The rhinos lurched about as they pulled at the grasses around them.

'Woolly rhinos,' Ralph said wonderingly. 'They're, like, from the Ice Age. How are they here?'

His only response was from one of the woolly rhinos. It toppled onto its side and gave a keening cry of agony, beating its head against the ground as its legs twitched. It was having some kind of seizure. Robyn's heart went out to it.

'What's wrong with it?' said Luke.

'Well, for a start, it's been extinct for fifteen thousand years,' Ralph said. He paused. 'It went extinct about the same time as the cave lion. This is like a live-action version of *Predasaur*.'

'Are you doing some kind of promotion deal here with the video game?' Luke asked uneasily. 'Could be a real money-spinner. If Mr Gerhard needs investors, my dad owns VanRok Security. I bet he'd chip in. I only came here to show Mr Gerhard what our software can do – see if he wants to invest, you know?'

Subtle, Luke, thought Robyn.

Abi didn't react or say a word. She steered away from the savannah and the woolly rhinos were soon lost from sight.

Robyn's mind was racing. No wonder Gerhard kept the place so private; he'd opened his own wild window on the ancient past. But why? She supposed that a 'Predasaur Park' *would* be an amazing tourist attraction. President Mbato would surely back that if it brought visitors from all over the world to spend money here – and that could explain his namecheck in Stefan's note. What else had it said?

Genetic engineering . . . trophy hunting . . . Predasaur killing . . .

Robyn thought of the cave lion and the sick woolly rhino, both with bloodied eyes, and knew in her gut that something way darker was going on here. Before the laws on trophy hunting had changed, so many safari parks used to promise hunters the ultimate goal: a chance to bring down the Big Five game animals – lion, leopard, rhino, elephant and buffalo. Maybe Gerhard had used genetic engineering to create an Even Bigger Five here. Designer animals bred for one thing – to be killed and posed with. If it had no impact on numbers in the wild, the scheme was technically . . .

Fair game, Robyn thought with a shudder.

They drove for almost an hour through Gerhard's game reserve in sullen, sweaty silence. Finally, they crowned a hill and Robyn found herself looking down over a complex of single- and double-storey stuccoed buildings with red roofs, connected by tarmac paths. It was an unimposing place, looking more like a university campus than the sort of ultra-modern villainous lair she'd imagined. She saw two uniformed wardens escorting a young man around Luke's age and a woman towards a concrete outbuilding. The woman looked unkempt and browbeaten, and the young man had a deep gash on his cheek.

They looked like prisoners.

Ralph had noticed them too. 'Are those two here on a day trip?'

Abi spared him the briefest of glances. 'I think they're interested in the hunting opportunities we can offer.'

Then Robyn saw an enormous animal enclosure close to the main buildings, like a sort of zoo. Three huge hairy animals were hemmed in by a concrete wall topped with wire, with a moat running around it.

At first glance, they looked like elephants. But then, the rhinos had just looked like rhinos . . .

'Oh my God,' Robyn breathed.

Each had a head as big as an armchair, with a wide, flattened forehead and a gigantic trunk. Their tusks were huge – they had to be three metres long, Robyn estimated, and curved outwards from their jaws in an enormous ivory arc. The animals were moving restlessly, shifting back and forth, seeming to be in discomfort, flicking their trunks.

'Mammoths,' Luke said simply. '*Woolly mammoths*, for God's sake.'

As the jeep came closer, Robyn intended to scrutinise the dark, shaggy fur that covered the animals; instead, the nearest mammoth's eyes caught her attention. They held the same raw redness as the cave lion and rhino's eyes, as if they were ready to burst.

Usually she could tell something at least about how an animal felt, create some sort of communication with them, but looking into the eyes of this animal, she could tell . . . nothing. The mammoth's mood was as enigmatic as its existence. She couldn't reach it in any way. The understanding that she had had for almost her whole life was missing with these strange, out-of-time creatures. She felt hollow, incomplete.

'Look at their ivory,' Ralph said quietly. 'It would fetch a fortune.'

'Yes,' Robyn whispered back. *And some billionaire is going to kill the beast it belongs to, take a trophy photo next to its body, and leave with modern-day mammoth ivory as his souvenir.*

'Even if it's worth millions, it has to cost as much to make one of those things,' said Luke. 'I mean . . . science, right?'

'Right,' said Ralph.

The jeep turned away from the animal enclosure and the ride became smooth as they joined a tarmacked path.

'Sorry I can't give you more of a guided tour,' Abi said

drily as she parked beside Beardy's jeep in front of one of the low, stucco buildings. 'But I know Shrinker's eager to begin.'

'Out you get,' said the warden next to Ralph, climbing out of the jeep, his Taser already in his hand.

Beardy had gone up to the big, black door in the wall and pressed his thumb against an entry coder. The door clicked open.

'Do go in,' said Beardy with a smile.

Robyn, Luke and Ralph were pushed through the doorway. Motion sensors triggered the lights, which flicked on. The walls were bare concrete; the room looked like another animal enclosure.

'Make yourselves comfortable,' said Beardy, and slammed the door on them. The smell of bleach caught in Robyn's nostrils. It smelled as if the place had recently been cleaned. The floor was marked with dark stains.

It's just damp, Robyn told herself, and tried very hard to believe it. *We've been caught, roughed up and shoved in a makeshift cell.*

What's next?

12

Ralph didn't hear the door lock, but the scuff of boots on gravel just outside told him that wardens were guarding the door.

'Well,' said Luke. 'This sucks.'

'Big time,' Ralph agreed. 'They've really got us.'

'Yeah,' Robyn whispered. 'D'you think they know we've recor—'

'*Recalled* Dad from that work trip he was on, so he'll be looking for us?' Ralph broke in noisily and tapped his ear, hoping she'd get the message: *Stay quiet about the evidence. Chances are, they're listening in.* He couldn't see any cameras, but that didn't mean there weren't hidden eyes and ears on them. 'Well, they'll find out soon enough.'

'I guess they will.' Robyn nodded, walking over to Luke. 'How is your sting doing now?'

'Still hurts like hell,' Luke said, looking pleased that Robyn was showing him some sympathy. Really it was just a way for her to get close enough to whisper, 'Keep quiet and act dumb – about everything.'

'It's a good job there's nothing dumb about the VanRok encryption on our phones,' Luke murmured. 'Good luck to them trying to break through *that* security.'

Ralph nodded. 'I wish I hadn't lost my phone *and* my gun,' he said clearly. 'The drone came out of nowhere. I was going to shine the phone torch into its lens to confuse it, but dropped it as I ran.'

Then a distant scream rang out, followed by a woman's voice. 'Leave him alone!' She said it with such desperation, Ralph felt a chill go through him.

Luke seemed rattled too. 'Rough neighbourhood, huh?' he joked weakly.

Then the door slammed open. Abi stood in the doorway. A middle-aged man with thinning hair and a dark beard pushed past her. He was stocky, with full features and a round face. He could have looked jolly, but an outdoor life had weathered his skin to leather and his eyes were hard. The smile he gave came nowhere close to kindness or sincerity.

'I'm Kurt Shrinker, Chief of Security at the Josef Gerhard Reserve.' He swung around to Abi, his air that of a teacher disappointed by a usually able pupil. 'Now, come on. Why were our unexpected visitors put in the veterinary enclosure, Abigail?'

Ralph was pleased to notice her discomfort.

'Well,' Abi began, 'we didn't think you'd want to –'

'These aren't hardened criminals,' Shrinker went on. 'Two of them are from just across the river. Neighbours, aren't you, eh?' He attempted a warmer smile, but it came out as more of a leer. 'I'm sure this is all a misunderstanding.'

'It is,' said Luke quickly. 'I'm Luke van Rok. My father's the CEO of VanRok –'

'Security. Yes, I know.' Shrinker's dark eyes turned on Luke. 'Although I take it you're not here in any professional capacity? I'm sorry for your treatment nonetheless. No hard feelings, I hope.'

'We're OK,' Robyn said. 'But we heard someone cry out.'

'Warden got injured,' Shrinker said casually. 'Don't worry, the wound won't bother him for long. Come through to a hospitality room.'

Luke smiled with relief. 'Really?'

'Thank you,' said Ralph.

'Well, we wouldn't want to upset your father, would we? The great Roland Ballantyne. He sounded quite agitated when we spoke yesterday.' Shrinker was still smiling. 'Abi, is Hospitality Suite Two available?'

She nodded unenthusiastically and pulled out a pass card. 'I'll get it opened up.'

Shrinker gestured for Ralph, Luke and Robyn to follow Abi out into the fading sunlight. Ralph felt uneasy about this change in treatment; he remembered the warden's warning to Abi when she'd gone to kick Robyn again. *Leave something for Shrinker.*

He fell into line behind his sister and Luke; appropriately, they formed a crocodile as they walked along tarmacked paths and between two stuccoed buildings to reach a third. Inside was a large meeting room, smart and functional. A row of metal chairs along the back wall gave the room an institutional feel, but a table by the door held bottles of water, a bowl of fruit and an unopened packet of Cape Cookies. There was a large infotainment screen attached to the wall on the other side of the room, with rolling headlines at the bottom of the screen. *MYSTERY VIRUS: MORE CASES CONFIRMED*, read one.

Then the virus wasn't contained at Gauda, Robyn thought grimly. All that violence, all the murders – for nothing. She wished she could ask about Stefan and how he'd caught the killer disease, but she didn't dare give away how much she knew already.

'Help yourself to refreshments,' Shrinker said, tossing a water bottle to Ralph, who caught it, and to Luke, who didn't (and who ostentatiously rubbed his sting by way of excuse). 'You've had quite a day. Tell me, what do you think of our enhanced animals? Prosthetics, holographic projection . . . they look like proper predasaurs, don't they?'

Ralph frowned. 'You mean that cave lion was just a regular lion in fancy dress?'

'It was convincing enough to scare the hell out of me,' said Robyn.

'I'm pleased to hear it, given what Mr Gerhard paid for the special effects,' Shrinker said.

'I could've been killed.'

'We weren't expecting intruders on set.'

Ralph swigged deeply from the bottle, the cool water soothing his parched throat. 'Set?' he queried.

'You disrupted a professional shoot,' Shrinker went on.

'A shoot! Right,' Luke said, as if light were dawning. 'Yeah, we saw the hunters.'

'Not that kind of shoot. A *movie* shoot.' Shrinker chuckled. '*Predasaur X*.'

'You mean, the cutscenes in *Predasaur* are motion-captured from live-action film?' Ralph had to admit, Shrinker's story *sounded* as though it explained a lot. 'How involved is Mr Gerhard in *Predasaur*?'

'Don't you know?' Shrinker said blandly. 'He holds a controlling interest in the companies that make it. Executive control over the whole thing.'

If I'd known that, I'd never have played it, Ralph thought. But he kept his face neutral. 'So, rather than enhance the footage using computers, you actually make up the animals to look prehistoric?'

'We're looking to open a *Predasaur* safari park,' Shrinker said, biting into an apple, all relaxed. 'Creating our "extinct" animals is a hell of a process, but Mr Gerhard figures the results are worth it.'

'Worth one of our bull elephants on *our* land being torn apart?' said Robyn coldly. 'Worth maiming one of our lions?'

Shrinker held up his hands in a *you-got-me* gesture. 'Some of the animals don't always take direction so well, and one of them became a bit . . . independent. Mr Gerhard will be pleased to reimburse you for your loss.'

'Money won't let Jari hunt again,' Robyn snapped.

'And it won't help that dude we saw killed at the river,' Luke said, even as Robyn flashed him a serious glare. 'But, uh . . . if that was just a movie shoot, then I guess he wasn't really dead?'

'Course not. He was a stuntman. Directed over in-ear headphones. He dived and released a dummy from under the water.' Shrinker looked at the three of them in turn. 'Sounds like you got a pretty good look at the action down by the river, huh?'

'It was great, bruh,' Luke began.

'Glad you think so. We had some big names for this shoot. All top-secret, of course, till it's announced officially.' Shrinker's smile died on his lips. 'Did you see anyone you think you recognised?'

Ralph suddenly realised what was happening. Shrinker wasn't just making conversation. He was fishing to find out how much they knew, feeding them the story about the movie set to see if they disagreed with him. 'We were too far away to see,' he said. 'But I said that guy had to be a stuntman, didn't I, Rob?'

'Yeah, and I knew the drones had to be filming it,' Robyn agreed firmly. She'd caught on too. 'Like I guess they film your fake mammoths and woolly rhinos – for your upcoming safari park, right?'

'World-class landscape, world-class FX,' Shrinker said proudly. '*Predasaur*'s got to keep ahead of the pack, right? The realism is part of why it's so successful. So Mr Gerhard has to protect his intellectual property from spies – and his territory from deliberate trespassers. Doesn't he, eh?'

'Please, Mr Shrinker,' said Robyn, wishing she'd been a little less hostile earlier. 'We only wanted to return one of Mr Gerhard's springbok and ask about the animal that had come onto our land – and whoever came after it. Our dad couldn't get through to Mr Gerhard and we thought the animals here could be in danger too.'

Shrinker nodded and handed her a bottle of water. 'You care a lot about animals.'

'You can see we cared for that springbok,' Robyn said, taking the water. 'We really were trying to do the right thing. We just got carried away at the chance to explore a bit.'

'If we promise not to do it again,' said Ralph, 'can we just go home?'

'It'll be all right, son.' Shrinker pulled Robyn's phone from his own pocket and passed it to her. 'Why don't you call your dad and tell him where you are.'

Robyn took the phone. A sudden fear fired shots in Ralph's mind. *He wants her to unlock the phone*, he realised. *Not so she can phone Dad – so he can see what we filmed.*

'There's no point trying Dad,' Ralph said quickly. 'He's out of town.'

'Leave him a message.' Shrinker smiled at Ralph. 'The man who patted you down didn't find your phone.'

'I lost it in the park when one of your drones dived at me.'

'Don't worry, we'll find it,' Shrinker assured him.

Robyn held the phone awkwardly. 'I've got no signal here.'

'Open it up,' Shrinker cajoled her. 'I'll connect you to the wifi here.'

Robyn shook her head. 'Dad will be so mad when he finds out we've done this without telling him. I don't need the aggro.'

'Why don't *you* call Mr Ballantyne, bruh?' Luke suggested. 'Though he's gone to meet up with his old army mates so he probably won't pick up . . .'

Ralph flashed him a *shut up* look, but it was too late.

'Meeting old army mates, eh?' Shrinker's pale blue eyes were cold as glaciers as he looked between Ralph and Robyn. 'Reunion with the Recces, is it?'

'We don't know,' said Ralph.

'You don't, huh?' Shrinker shook his head impatiently. 'Well, the hell with this. Who needs the hassle? You broke through two security checkpoints into an area you know damn well is off-limits to the public, with high-powered binoculars and a sat-phone with HD video capability. Snooping. Spying.' He snatched Robyn's phone from her, put it into his pocket.

'Hey!' Robyn began.

He took out his own phone. 'I'm calling the cops. I'll let them deal with you.' Dialling a number, Shrinker threw open the door. He powered through and it slammed shut behind him.

'You'd better get your phone back, Rob,' Luke said. 'If we don't have that video of the killer croc tearing through those hunters, we have nothing to show for this.'

'Quiet!' Ralph mouthed. They might still be overheard. Then he raised his voice. 'You know those weren't real hunters . . .'

'We are in such trouble. Big, big, big trouble.' Luke threw up his arms in disgust and stomped over to one of the chairs by the refreshments table. He tried to pull it away from the wall, but it wouldn't budge. 'What the hell? It's bolted to the floor!'

Robyn looked at Ralph. 'Chairs fixed to the floor for casual chit-chat over biscuits and fruit? Doesn't make sense.'

Ralph nodded, feeling his heart sink. *Shrinker's played us. Put us in here and cranked up the pressure, trying to get us to spill the little details. Then he walked out so we'd talk about it together – and spill the big ones.* In that second, Ralph guessed that Shrinker had not gone to call the police. That they weren't going to get off with a trip to the station and a dressing-down from the desk sergeant.

Abruptly the door swung open. A tall man in a hat with a curved brim stepped inside. He wore a grey three-piece suit that set him apart from Shrinker and the khaki-clad rangers. The man's face was fiercely aristocratic, clean-shaven, with icy grey eyes that bulged behind round pebble spectacles. He smiled, white teeth bared like any other predator.

Ralph recognised the man at once. It was Josef Gerhard.

13

Gerhard's appearance caught Robyn off-balance. She'd seen the man a hundred times in the news and online, but to see him in person . . . it was like coming face to face with a bogeyman you'd been told about since childhood.

'So, you didn't believe the cover story about us faking the action down by the river.' Gerhard shook his head sadly. 'A pity. If you'd swallowed it, we might have let you go.'

Shrinker and Abi followed Gerhard into the room and stood behind him.

'You really have brought extinct animals back to life, then,' Ralph said quietly. 'We knew Shrinker was lying.'

'A little respect for Mr Shrinker, please,' said Gerhard. 'He's a former British SAS officer who has shifted into . . . private security.'

'Pays better,' Shrinker said. 'That's no lie.'

'So why are you really here – two Ballantynes and the son and heir to the VanRok Security empire?' Gerhard wondered aloud. 'Come to borrow a cup of sugar?'

'We didn't think you were even home,' Ralph said. 'Dad said he'd tried to get hold of you –'

'I guess I should ring him back.' Gerhard's smile was as frigid as an icebox. 'We can talk about how he can help me now. After all, I've kept his precious children alive after they put themselves in danger.'

Robyn decided that calm politeness was the best policy. 'Like we've said all along, we only wanted to return your springbok.'

'I've had that ewe picked up.' Gerhard gave an over-the-top grin. 'Thanks, good neighbour!'

'And,' Robyn went on quickly, 'we wanted to warn you that she was nearly killed by something that got onto our land . . . and could've got on to yours.'

'Sadly, the sarcosuchus has proved hard to recapture after chewing its way through the boundary nets in the river,' said Gerhard. 'I regret the incursions onto your land, but I'm sure you'd rather we at least tried to retrieve it. See? You're a good neighbour to me, and I'm a good neighbour to you.' He hefted Robyn's phone in his hand. 'And good neighbours watch out for each other. So, with your personal safety in mind, I have to say . . . if you've taken any pictures or video of some of the more dramatic moments from today's events at the riverbank, I suggest you delete them. Now.'

'Mr Gerhard?' Ralph looked him right in the eye. 'I swear to you that there are no videos or photos on that phone.'

'He's right,' said Robyn, thrusting her chin out.

'You can smash it if you like,' Ralph went on.

Robyn glanced at him uncertainly.

'Yeah,' Luke said. 'Evidence or not, it doesn't matter if you break the handset. Auto-archive software backs up the entire camera roll to the cloud.'

'He's lying, sir,' Shrinker sneered. 'Your security sats block all signals coming out of the park.'

'That's only true if you have fibre-optic links all across the reserve,' Luke said calmly. 'And that's not easy in a big old park, right? You must share bandwidth from third-party satellites to connect to the world outside.'

'That's right. But on a secure network,' Gerhard agreed.

'VanRok tech is great at hacking into secure networks,' Luke informed him. 'How else did we get in here?'

Robyn stared at Luke, not sure if he was helping things or not. But she was pleased to see Gerhard turn expectantly to Abi, and the discomfort on the woman's face.

'It's possible that data got out,' she said reluctantly. 'There's always some spectrum overlap between GEO and NGEO satellites which can cause blind spots –'

'All right, Abigail, you can spare us the technical details.' Gerhard remained calm as he looked at the phone in his hand. 'Well. It's a useful lesson, I suppose: all things can be broken.' He looked at Robyn with those bulging grey eyes. 'Can't they?'

Robyn refused to give him the satisfaction of seeing she was afraid. 'Why does our being here even matter to you?' she asked. 'If you're recreating prehistoric animals, you must plan to go public sometime.'

'At a time of my choosing,' Gerhard agreed. 'The power to return extinct animals to life belongs to me.'

'But you bring them back to life just so you can shoot them,' Ralph muttered. 'That's sick. And it's illegal. Trophy hunting is banned.'

'These are modified creatures created in a private lab at great expense.' Gerhard smiled coolly. 'Since they belong to me, I can do whatever I want with them.'

Robyn sneered. 'You've turned these animals into things. Objects for you to use.'

'Why the red eyes?' Luke asked.

'A minor imbalance in the genetic code that causes inflammation in the uvea – the middle layer of the eyeball,' said Gerhard. 'I considered correcting it, but it does give the creatures a distinctive look, don't you think?'

'They're in pain,' Robyn snapped.

'The pain makes them more aggressive,' said Gerhard. 'As far as I'm concerned, that's a good thing: I have created the ultimate game. The more dangerous the hunt, the bigger the thrill.'

'Wait,' Ralph said. 'The ultimate game – that's the slogan for *Predasaur*.'

Gerhard seemed pleased by Ralph's observation. 'Appropriate, don't you think? Considering that sales of *Predasaur* have helped fund this project – and elements of the project have helped *Predasaur* feel more real. Each feeds on the other. A feeding frenzy, you might say.' He flexed his shoulders, savouring the moment. 'My discoveries will change the world.'

'But not for the better,' Robyn murmured.

'I can see that you have been well indoctrinated by your father,' said Gerhard. 'You're young, you're supposed to be looking to the future – to how things are going to be. Your father is a dinosaur. Out of date. *Wrong*.'

'Prove it,' said Robyn.

Ralph and Luke looked at her like she was crazy.

'You want to see what evidence is on this phone, but you can't get past the security, can you?' Robyn tried to keep cool. 'Well, convince us that you're right and Dad's wrong – and then I'll unlock the phone.'

'Robyn,' Ralph began. 'What are you do –'

'You want to wait until they start threatening us properly? They'll get what they're after in the end.' Robyn hoped her despair was convincing enough for Gerhard to buy it. If they could only get out of this cell and into the grounds, perhaps they had a chance of escape. 'No one has to get hurt. Convince us you're right, Mr Gerhard, and we'll do whatever you want. We'll make Dad see he's been wrong to fight you all this time.'

Cold silence met her words. Gerhard's spreading smile did little to warm it. 'Roland Ballantyne's own children telling him that I'm right and he isn't! That's amusing.' His smile faded. 'Very well. A small tour of my facility can be arranged. Let's take a walk together, shall we?' He turned and walked out the door. Abi grabbed Robyn's arm and led her out as Shrinker took charge of Ralph and Luke.

It had grown dark outside. Robyn looked up at the moon and the stars. They shone down as distant as always, but safety felt a lot further away.

14

Ralph hadn't expected to find a super-advanced lab complex deep inside a game reserve. Gerhard was leading them along a white corridor with a series of large plate-glass windows along one side. He stopped so that they could all admire the domain beyond, though Abi and Shrinker took little notice. Both looked ill at ease in this high-tech world, away from the simple rules of the natural world outside.

Gerhard, on the other hand, was apparently revelling in having Roland Ballantyne's children in his power. Ralph realised that Robyn had tried to play on Gerhard's vanity – and sense of how wronged the man must feel. *A villain never thinks he's the villain*, Roland had told Ralph once, talking about his military days. *He can always justify his actions. As far as he's concerned, the world's just too stupid to see things his way.*

Robyn had bought them time. But with Shrinker and Abi always hovering, the threat of violence was never far away.

Ralph was fascinated by the lab, despite himself. Everything on the other side of the glass looked shiny and smooth, and floors curved where they met the walls rather than joining at a 90-degree angle: all was easy to clean and keep sterilised. The door at the end of the corridor had a viewing panel, and Ralph could see into the airlock-style entrance to the lab. The airlock was lined with lockers and rows of lab coats and clean gowns on hooks.

Ralph took a closer look at the edge of one window and saw that the frame held three separate sheets of glass, each sealed to prevent any possible contamination. He had the weirdest feeling that he'd been here before – then remembered that one of the levels in *Predasaur* took place in a ruined lab building. The layout was different but he felt a strange, uncomfortable thrill as he recognised some of the details – the freezers, the biological safety cabinets and incubators. Just how much of *Predasaur* had been inspired by reality?

Lab staff in white coveralls and masks were moving about inside the lab, testing biological samples.

'Are they de-extincting animals in there right now?' Robyn asked. 'What's next – a sabre-toothed tiger? A terror bird? A herd of giant elks for them to feed on?'

'Wait,' Ralph said. 'The cave lion, the mammoths, woolly rhinos – they're all mammals, and all quite recent. They went extinct fifteen . . . thirty thousand years ago.'

'That's not recent!' Luke spluttered.

'Compared to a sarcosuchus it is,' Ralph pointed out. 'And it's, like, related to crocodiles. It's a reptile.'

'Sarcosuchus was the first breakthrough,' Gerhard explained. 'I can't claim the credit. It was the result of research that I bought from a Danish company. They took a crocodile and undid the evolutions in its DNA to create a more primitive creature that merely *resembles* a sarcosuchus.' He began to remind Ralph of the worst of his tutors, holding forth on his pet subject. 'I have built on that research to make true recreations of extinct beasts. But DNA decays over time and none has been known to last longer than a million years. Finding enough cells from an extinct species as well as a suitable source of recipient egg cells and surrogate mothers has posed a serious challenge.'

'Surrogate mothers,' Robyn echoed. 'You mean, like elephants giving birth to woolly mammoths, cos they're sort of similar?'

Gerhard jumped as if stung, clearly not used to being interrupted. 'Yes, Robyn. For instance, our cave lion embryo was implanted inside an African lioness.'

Ralph swallowed hard. 'And she gave birth to that . . . monster?'

'With a good deal of help,' said Gerhard. 'We use a mixture of techniques – cross-species cloning, some genetic modifications, careful application of MicroRNA to recreate desired characteristics . . .'

'You're going to a lot of effort with these things,' said Robyn, 'just to try and kill them.'

'They are permitted to kill too, under controlled conditions,' Gerhard informed her. 'The cutscene animations in *Predasaur* are based on actual recorded footage that we then enhance.'

Ralph felt sick. 'You mean, the sarcosuchus actually killed

real people while you watched – and you put that in the game?'

Stefan had summed it up perfectly in his note: *PREDASAUR KILLING.*

'Motion capture,' Luke blurted, looking at Ralph. 'Handled by Q-Base Holosoft, right? The same people that made the chip in the springbok . . .' He trailed off under Gerhard's icy glare.

'What a keen eye the young have,' Gerhard said. 'I own Q-Base Holosoft, as I own all the companies that make *Predasaur* the success it is. And I take a very close personal interest in their work. You could call *Predasaur* . . . my passion project. Sarcosuchus has already appeared in several versions of the game, and we must keep the franchise fresh with new beasts.'

'So now you've used it, it's OK to kill it?' Robyn couldn't keep the disgust off her face. 'I guess if you breed these things to be in constant pain, it's a mercy killing.'

'What else are we to do with such creatures?' Gerhard shrugged. 'Left alone in the wild, their hunger would empty my reserve.'

'And ours,' Ralph added. 'You couldn't contain it, could you? It got loose.'

'Accidents happen,' said Gerhard airily. 'But I am engineering replacements. Come on, I'll show you.' He led the way back down the corridor and out of the building. With a worried look at his sister and Luke, Ralph followed, Shrinker and Abi at his back.

* * *

129

Robyn smelled the warm earthiness of animal pens as they entered a warehouse-sized building. Once again, there was no clear way out. No chance to escape. She wasn't sure how much longer she could keep up her front of keen interest. Everything Gerhard was doing here made her want to run away screaming. He must know she would never turn against her father . . .

But once Gerhard tired of showing off his cleverness . . . what then?

Gerhard led the way onto a raised walkway overlooking pens of different sizes. Each was barred like a jail cell, accessed from a wide walkway big enough to accommodate barrels of feed. She saw keepers moving about with food supplies and other equipment, but her attention soon shifted to the animals themselves.

Two jaguar cubs were play-fighting in the pen directly below. *No*, Robyn realised. Not jaguar cubs. They had stocky forelimbs, bulky forequarters and sturdy muscles; here was some other animal throwback. One of them glanced up, attracted by the movement on the walkway, and Robyn saw that its eyes were weeping red too.

'Tigers?' Luke asked.

'Megantereon,' Gerhard said smugly, as if he'd just cooked and served an exotic meal. 'A sabre-toothed cat that prowled the savannah five hundred thousand years ago.' He started down a metal staircase towards the enclosures. 'Just think. Early man, *homo erectus*, once competed with these beasts for prey. Spear against tooth. Survival the only prize.'

'Horrible,' Ralph muttered. 'But it's not like they were killing just for sport.'

'I'm glad you appreciate the difference,' said Shrinker, and shared a smirk with Abi.

What's so funny? Robyn wondered with a shiver of apprehension.

Gerhard led them on to the next pen. This one held what looked like five hyenas, but their faces were twisted, malformed. They were limping back and forth as though they were unable to settle. Their eyes were red and twitching, and Robyn felt a prickle of discomfort raise the hairs on the back of her neck. 'Are these in *Predasaur* too?'

Ralph moved up next to her. 'No,' he said, chewing his lip. 'Not yet, at least.'

'Cave hyenas,' said Gerhard grandly. 'Concocted from partial DNA almost fifteen thousand years old.'

'Bigger than regular hyenas,' Luke noted.

Abi smirked. 'Big enough to drag their kills to their lair rather than eating out in the open.'

I need a stronger stomach. Robyn shut her eyes, thinking about the grim future that these animals faced. *We're all in the same boat.* She wondered if the animals knew they were different; if they sensed that they'd been created to die, and that fed into their blind aggression. *Gerhard can stitch his own animals from modern tech and ancient DNA*, she thought, *but he can never give them souls.*

The next pen was larger, giving Robyn a good look at the woolly rhinos that they had only glimpsed earlier from the back of Gerhard's truck. This one held a mother and two young rhinos. The youngsters were almost covered in pale grey fur that had a faint red-pink tint and were already showing the stumps of their two horns, while the mother was a more subdued grey-brown. Each had the same familiar raw, bloodshot eyes as the rest of Gerhard's menagerie.

'These are seven months old,' said Gerhard, just behind her. 'They'll go out to join the herd soon.' He turned to Luke. 'Can you imagine bagging one of them when it's full grown, boy?'

'I've not done any hunting,' Luke admitted, then quickly added: 'I mean, I'm interested, but . . .'

'The moment you know you've killed a beast like this is truly magical,' Gerhard assured him, rapt. 'Any dangerous-game hunter will agree. Something from old and primitive times instinctively rises inside you to taste the pleasure of the kill . . .'

'You're sick!' Robyn blurted, then bit her lip.

'You'll never see things my way,' Gerhard said quietly. 'Your sentimentality stops you seeing life as it's meant to be – the primal desire not just to survive, but to *dominate*.'

'No,' Robyn began, trying to backtrack. 'I . . . I really am starting to see where you're coming from –'

'It's where you're going to that you should consider now,' Gerhard said. 'Don't worry, the guided tour hasn't ended yet. Would you like to get a little closer to my animals – appreciate the craftsmanship up close?'

Abi suddenly appeared next to Robyn and wrapped a firm hand around her upper arm.

'Get off me,' Robyn snapped. But as she tried to pull free, Shrinker grabbed her other arm.

'Let go of her!' said Ralph, stepping forward.

Shrinker turned and shoved him aside, sending him sprawling against the bars. 'Don't make a fuss now, eh?' he breathed. 'She's good with animals, right?'

The animals in the pen began to whine and growl. Two keepers ran over, alerted by the scuffle. Luke quickly helped Ralph up, and the keepers blocked their way, preventing them from reaching Robyn.

'Robyn, wait,' said Gerhard as Abi started to lead her away.

Robyn looked back at him, her heart in her throat, clutching at any chance of reprieve.

'I'm going to give you your phone back.' Gerhard pressed it into her hand as Abi and Shrinker escorted her down a flight of whitewashed steps. 'You might like to take photographs, hmm?'

The air was rank with the musky stink of animal as Shrinker and Abi led her into a larger enclosure. It was divided in two by a gate-like barrier. She saw Luke and Ralph, restrained by the keepers, watching with Gerhard from the walkway above. Shrinker and Abi stepped out and closed the metal-barred door, shutting her in. Leaving Abi to watch her, Shrinker stalked off into the shadows.

Robyn stayed very still in the gloom, trying to control her breathing. She couldn't afford to be flustered. She had to remain calm.

'Now,' said Gerhard, his voice carrying down to her and

echoing off the concrete wall. 'You kindly offered to unlock your phone if I could convince you I was right about the future. Well, believe me, your future is going to be terribly brief if you don't show me the evidence you've captured right now.'

'Why does it matter to you?' Robyn shouted. 'You've shown us everything anyway.'

'I've shared with you my knowledge,' Gerhard agreed. 'Now share yours. Unlock the phone.'

Robyn tapped the screen. There was no signal and the battery was low. If only it would run out right now! 'I . . . I can't remember my passcode.'

'I suggest you try.'

A few moments later, Robyn heard a noise from the adjoining pen. She looked up from the phone screen and saw Shrinker at the other side of the pen, standing next to a keeper. The door at the far side of the enclosure opened and a huge, shaggy beast was forced inside, dragging its chain, which trailed from a metal collar.

To Robyn's horror, it was a full-grown sabretooth. The ones she'd seen from the walkway above were cubs, but this one was at least a year older, quite capable of hunting and with its huge canine teeth grown in. It had tell-tale red eyes underneath a huge, primitive brow. Its breath came in bubbling rasps, as if it hurt to breathe.

And the pain made it angry.

The sabretooth prowled back and forth, back and forth, staring at her each time it passed the gate. Thick, bloody drool fell from the ivory fangs curving down from its jaws.

Robyn tried to slow her breathing and settle her mind, praying that she could make some sort of connection with the sabretooth. But the beast banged its head against the gate separating them and gave a chilling roar. Its red eyes were dull and clouded. It forced a thick, twisted forelimb through the bars, swiping the air with murderous claws.

'Get her out of there!' Ralph shouted.

'Come on, Mr Gerhard,' Luke tried more politely. 'A joke's a joke, right?'

'No joke, Robyn,' Gerhard called down. 'I'd rather not deliver you back to your heartbroken father in a pizza box, so please unlock the phone.'

Robyn felt panic wash through her again. This wasn't Jari or Sabal; she couldn't reach out to the sabretooth on any level. The space where its proud, wild spirit should have soared was filled only with pain and cruelty and rage.

'This tiger has been trained on live bait and I am running out of patience,' Gerhard went on. 'So, if you would be so kind . . .'

Abi pulled a rope attached to a pulley outside the cage. The barrier separating Robyn from the big cat began to move slowly upwards.

'All right!' Robyn shouted and stabbed a shaking finger at the touchscreen. 'All right, I'll open it.'

'Don't do it, Rob!' Ralph yelled.

'If she doesn't,' said Shrinker, 'you're going in too.'

'I have to do this, Ralph!' she shouted back.

Ralph groaned. 'But you can't!'

The sabretooth snarled and started to scrabble under the widening gap, its hooked claws extended. It obviously knew what came next. As carefully as she could, despite her shaking hands, Robyn tapped the code to unlock her phone.

Nothing happened.

'Something's wrong – it won't open!' she shrieked, frantically trying again as Abi heaved again on the rope and the barrier rose higher still. The sabretooth was biting at the bars. It was strong, fast and heavy. The sound of its claws scraping on the bars knifed into Robyn's skull as she stabbed at the screen. Panic rose inside her. Nothing was working: she couldn't get through to the sabretooth and she couldn't unlock her own phone. Every option was dead to her. 'I'm serious, I can't get in!'

'She's telling the truth,' came Ralph's voice from above, tight and shrill. 'It's . . . the security settings on our family network.'

'Come off it,' sneered Shrinker.

'Interference between the phone and the data cloud must be blocking the login settings,' Luke said. 'It won't open till the phone is physically connected with their home mainframe again.'

'He's right,' Ralph said. 'More VanRok tech. Dad set it up.'

'Now, come on, let her go!' Luke shouted.

Abi was holding the barrier where it was, but the sabretooth had grown tired of waiting. It forced its way under the metal gate with a roar that could cut rock. Robyn clenched her teeth to stop herself screaming. She couldn't run. She had to look confident, show no fear. She couldn't be *prey*.

'Shrinker!' Abi yelled, dropping the barrier back into place so she could draw her Taser. A few moments later, a slew of blue crackles burst over the sabretooth's chest, and it roared and recoiled. At the same time, Robyn dodged forward and aimed a roundhouse kick at the sabretooth's throat. *Dominate it*, she thought, *meet its aggression head-on*. It flinched and paused, staring at her with those unearthly red eyes.

Then there was a scrabbling as Shrinker pushed open the door to the pen and hurled in a live springbok. In a slow-motion moment, Robyn saw the healing wound on its flank and realised it was the ewe that they'd rescued and brought back to the Gerhard Reserve. The ewe's dark eyes were wide as it turned to her and, at once, Robyn's heart was snatched back to the moment she'd first found the injured springbok: sensing the ewe's hurt and fear. The first quiet stirrings of trust.

She barely had time to scream before the tiger pounced on the stunned ewe. Moaning with pain that wasn't hers, Robyn stumbled blindly to the barred door and felt rough hands grab her and pull her through.

She collapsed against the wall of the corridor, sobbing and empty. She'd never experienced such a connection with an animal at the moment of its death. That instinctive link must have been heightened by stress and fear. *I saved her life back in the park*, Robyn thought dully. *And she saved mine.*

Dimly, she heard noises. She opened her eyes and lifted her head as the world came back into focus around her. She heard Ralph shouting her name. 'Robyn! Are you all right?'

The phone slipped from her hand and hit the concrete. Shrinker scooped it up.

Abi took Robyn's arm and steered her back up the steps. It was all Robyn could do to stop her legs from buckling under her, but she made it to the top and stared into Gerhard's hateful face.

'That almost got out of hand, didn't it?' Brightness danced in his bulging eyes as Gerhard snatched the phone from Shrinker. 'Phew!'

'You didn't have to kill the ewe,' Robyn said.

'It was the nearest meat to hand,' Shrinker replied. 'Don't worry, there are loads exactly like it. It's only a clone.'

Ralph stared. 'What?'

'Fifth-generation clone,' said Luke. 'We thought that meant the software on the chip.'

'But it meant the springbok,' Ralph breathed.

'I can undo extinction for long-dead species and you're shocked when I clone something as simple as a springbok?' Gerhard sneered. 'My beasts have large appetites. Why wait for infants to grow when I can simply clone their mothers?'

'In any case,' said Shrinker, 'Ralph here wanted a reward for helping that springbok and bringing her back. He got his sister back in one piece – does that cover it?'

Robyn wished she could slap him, but she was dizzy. Black spots dotted her vision as Abi gripped her wrist and twisted it behind her back.

'Please,' said Ralph hoarsely. 'Stop all this.'

'Yeah,' said Luke. 'Let us all go, and we'll get you the evidence. We won't say a word about anything that's happened here.'

Gerhard will never let us go, thought Robyn as her dizziness grew worse. *But why? What does he think we've got on him?*

Then her legs buckled, Robyn collapsed, and the world blinked out.

15

Ralph looked at Robyn, limp as a doll in Shrinker's arms, as the stocky soldier carried her up a flight of steps in the complex.

Abi was pushing Luke along while Beardy the ranger had joined them, one hand on Ralph's shoulder to steer him. Gerhard strolled behind them, Robyn's phone still in his hand.

'She needs an ambulance,' Ralph said. 'We need to get her to a hospital.'

'She fainted, is all,' Shrinker retorted. 'She can sleep it off in the staff sick bay and you can keep her company for the night.'

'Can I call my folks?' Luke asked. 'My dad's gonna flip out.'

'If you can open the girl's phone,' Abi said.

'Haven't you found mine in the reserve yet?' Ralph asked. 'I'll open that for you.'

'We'll find it,' Beardy assured him. 'Don't worry.'

Shrinker led the way onto a corridor and pushed open a grey door with a red cross printed in its middle. Inside was a small room with a tiny window set high in the wall. Shrinker dumped Robyn on a couch beside a rack of shelving heavy with medical supplies – latex gloves and face masks, bacterial wash and PPE. Ralph had thought that the most common injuries to staff would be caused by predasaurs, but this stuff . . .

It was more suited to coping with a virus.

Gerhard was frowning at Robyn's phone. 'Damn it, the thing's died. We'll have to find a charger.' He stalked out of the room.

Thank God for more time, thought Ralph. He smoothed Robyn's hair back from her cheek, not noticing Shrinker pull out his phone and aim it at the two of them. The camera shutter noise was loud in the quiet little space.

Ralph scowled. 'What was that?'

'Evidence.' Shrinker's grin was positively jolly. 'See, we can play that game too. Eh?'

'Sorry the tour was cut short,' Abi said as Beardy retreated outside. 'Don't worry, though. You'll be seeing more animals up close in the morning.'

The door closed and a heavy bolt shot home. Then three sets of footsteps moved away.

'I thought they'd never leave,' Luke joked nervously. 'Jeez, Ralph. These dudes are maniacs.'

'Like Frankenstein's vets.' Ralph nodded. 'At least they've given Robyn a couch to lie on.'

Luke was eyeing the shelves. 'There's enough medical supplies here to ride out a pandemic.'

'Or maybe to treat one at its source,' Ralph said

thoughtfully. 'Stefan got sick with that mystery virus after leaving here . . . Maybe it's not just animals they're making in those labs.'

'What a reassuring thought. Thanks for that, Ralph.' Luke surveyed the shelves. 'Think there's any ibuprofen? My arm still hurts from that sting.'

'Better than that,' said Ralph, shifting a box of plastic aprons aside. 'There's an air vent or something.' He pointed to a grille set into the wall close to floor level. 'It's kind of small, but I might just fit . . .'

Luke smiled. 'The door's locked from the outside with a thumb-turn bolt . . .'

'No key required,' Ralph concluded. 'So if I can get out somehow, I can unlock the door for you.'

'And we carry your sister to safety?' Luke snorted. 'Like we won't be caught straight away.'

Ralph glared at him. 'Do you have any better ideas?'

'They have to let us go, bruh,' Luke said, crossing to the window and staring out at the night-time shadows of the reserve. 'If we hold on long enough . . .'

'After what they've shown us, done to us, I can't see them letting us go.' Ralph sighed, trying to budge the grille. 'I don't understand why the evidence on the phone means so much to them when they've shown us everything up close anyway . . .' Then he swore. 'The screws are blind. Can't be removed without proper tools.'

Luke tried the window. The catch turned easily. '*This* opens.'

'Let's see.' Ralph pushed against the glass and the window

swung outward. 'If you help me up, I might just get out through there.'

'We're two storeys up!' Luke reminded him. 'If you fall, you'll break your neck.'

Ralph hesitated. 'Better that than ending up in a sabretooth's guts. Give me a leg up?' Luke made a stirrup with his hands and Ralph stepped into it. 'There's a ledge. I think I can reach it.'

'Famous last words,' said Luke. 'But if you can open the next-door window and get inside, you can unlock our door and off we go.'

Ralph licked his dry lips. 'Luke . . . if I don't come back, tell Robyn I'm sorry.' Struggling through the narrow window, he managed a last look back and a crooked smile. 'Sorry I left her with only you for company.'

Luke raised a finger. Ralph raised two, then turned the fingers round to suggest a peace sign – or V for victory. He wriggled through the window with some difficulty, trying to keep both feet on the narrow sill. Then he edged to the left and vanished.

Ralph had no luck forcing the window of the neighbouring room open; it refused to budge even a millimetre. But the upper storeys of the complex were clad with sheets of timber, and there were hand- and footholds enough to let him climb up onto the roof. From there, he reasoned, perhaps he could find a skylight, or an open window on the other side of the building.

The night was warm and filled with the calls and chitters of wildlife. Cold sweat outlined every aching muscle as he scrambled up the side of the complex and onto the flat roof. Once he got there, he wished he could just stay lying down, but he couldn't rest, not now. Too much was depending on this.

Ralph rose in a wary crouch and made his way across the roof. A kind of metal funnel rose up like a periscope near the middle, thrumming with the rumble of motors. It was the water-cooled chiller plant, and the pipes coming off it must lead to vents like the one in the sick bay. Perhaps he could get inside one and climb down into an unlocked room below?

He wrestled with the cover of the chiller unit, then stopped when he heard footsteps from the road next to the building. Holding his breath, Ralph made his way to the roof edge and peered over the low parapet.

A large, striking figure was walking along the dark pavement, which was lit with pools of orange from the streetlamps. With a heart like a grenade ready to blow, he recognised the man's jacket at once: emblazoned with crowned eagles, it marked him as the hunter who'd called the shots as well as fired them at the sarcosuchus back at the riverside.

Then Ralph saw the man's face.

It was the president: Julius Mbato.

Ralph almost swore out loud, then he heard Gerhard's voice as he strode out of the building to greet Mbato.

'Mr President! It's late.' Gerhard inclined his head. 'Main gate security told me you'd left the guest suite to meet me on foot . . .'

'I was tired of waiting,' Mbato rumbled.

'Forgive me. I had important business to attend to.' Gerhard paused. 'Anyway, I thought you'd returned to Pretoria after your hunting expedition this afternoon.'

'It ended dismally.'

Gerhard shrugged. 'I have no doubt your victory over the sarcosuchus will be all the sweeter for its frustrating your expectations.'

'I don't mean that,' snapped Mbato. 'I mean the intruders you let into your compound to take compromising videos of *me*.'

So that's why Gerhard's worked so hard to get what we filmed, Ralph realised. *We didn't see it at the time, squinting through the binoculars and filming on the little screen – but we were filming our beloved president!*

The president, illegally hunting an extinct monster while people died around him.

'As it happens,' Mbato went on, 'I did return to Pretoria. I've only come back here because of your mistakes.' He raised an expectant eyebrow. 'Have you secured the footage yet?'

'It's a matter of time,' Gerhard said calmly.

'A matter of time before the footage goes viral and my reputation's in tatters.'

'I think you're being overdramatic.'

'And if Roland Ballantyne *has* found his children's footage in the cloud?' Mbato sighed wearily. 'I followed up on what Shrinker learned from the Van Rok boy: Ballantyne and Xai have been cruising Pretoria, talking to old army colleagues – about Gauda. He must've figured out that the explosion was no accident. Not only that, but a sample of the virus has turned up at a biomedical company –'

'SangoMed?' Gerhard said quickly. 'Ballantyne's girlfriend works there. How the hell did she get a sample of the virus?'

'I don't know. Stefan's girlfriend, perhaps?'

'We've got her under lock and key with our other nuisances,' said Gerhard, 'and we've dealt with the doctor Stefan went to in Pretoria.'

'He's infected others. I've checked hospital admissions – they're up all across Pretoria. And the SangoMed tests will show that the virus isn't just zoonotic; it comes from an animal that no longer exists.' Mbato shook his head. 'The virus is dangerous to all age groups and highly transmissible. I'm almost certainly going to have to order a lockdown. The people don't like lockdowns, Gerhard. I need the people's votes for my third term in office – and you need me to *get* that third term if you want your plans to play out. And if what's happened here goes public, I'll bring you down with me.'

'Oh, Julius, for God's sake, relax.' Gerhard sounded petulant. 'Shrinker's secured all medical notes from the Gauda hospital and we're working to understand how the virus crossed over from the predasaurs. In the meantime, we have ways to keep Ballantyne *and* his girlfriend silent. We have the children.' Gerhard smiled and held up his phone. 'Shrinker took this picture not half an hour ago. I'm arranging for it to be sent to Ballantyne with an invitation to join us – alone.'

'He'll come, too,' Mbato mused. 'Always the hero.'

'Exactly.' Gerhard placed his hands on the president's

shoulders. 'Now, come on, Julius. I can see you need a drink. Stay tonight in my personal suite and join me for a hunt tomorrow morning.' They moved off, crossing the tarmac road together. 'Ballantyne will think he's racing to his children's rescue. What he doesn't know is . . .'

Ralph peered further over the parapet, hanging onto every word, but Gerhard and Mbato had disappeared through some double doors into the building opposite.

His head buzzing with all he'd just seen and heard, Ralph crossed back to the chiller plant and forced open the grille that protected the main pipe.

I've got to get Robyn and Luke out of here, he thought. *Somehow we've got to use our evidence to bring Mbato down – and Gerhard with him!*

16

Robyn woke from a deep, dark sleep, wondering where she was. For a few blissful moments she thought she was in her bed at home. Then the dreadful events she'd lived through rushed through her mind and she sat bolt upright.

'Whoa!' Luke cried, jumping up from the floor. His eyes were wet and he wiped them crossly. 'Uh . . . welcome back, Robyn.'

'Where are we?' She looked around. 'Are we safe?'

'No. This is Gerhard's sick bay. How you feeling now?'

'Horrible.' She put her face in her hands. 'That sabretooth . . . I thought I was going to die.'

'Yeah, well, the night is young.' Luke gave her a sorry smile and shuffled closer. 'Come on, it's all right. Want a hug? It would make me feel better, at least.'

'I guess,' said Robyn. But as Luke put his arms around her, she found she couldn't lean into the embrace. 'I'm sorry I got you into this.'

'Good,' Luke said, with a squeeze of her shoulder to show he wasn't totally serious.

'I really am sorry. I used you to get us in here, and now . . .'

'We just have to get out again. Right?'

'Right.' She froze suddenly. 'Wait. Where's Ralph?'

'He's getting us out,' Luke told her. 'He went out the window to find another way in so he can unlock that door and split.'

Robyn felt hope stir inside her. 'You think he can do it?'

'Maybe.'

Robyn kept her eyes on the door, listening for the slightest sound of someone approaching. But the noise, when it came, was a metallic shaking from behind the wall.

'The vent,' Luke realised. 'That must be Ralph! He's coming down the vent!'

'Luke?' came Ralph's weary voice through the wall. 'Is that you?'

'And me,' said Robyn. 'Are you all right?'

'I tried to get out into the corridor,' Ralph said. 'It was no good.'

Luke clutched his head and screwed up his eyes, his last hope gone.

'I've found some stuff out, though.' Ralph's voice grew louder as he inched through the shaft towards them. 'Things you won't believe. For a start, how tight these wingnuts have been put on the vent cover . . .'

'Oh God,' said Robyn.

'I'm not even joking,' Ralph murmured.

'Not that,' she hissed. 'Footsteps outside.'

'You're right. Someone's coming,' said Luke quietly. 'C'mon, Rob, let's get him out!'

She and Luke crouched down beside the vent cover, pulling

at it, trying to prise it open, while Ralph pushed against it with his feet. They knew they couldn't make too much noise.

'What's going on in there?' Abi called from the corridor.

'Hold the door shut!' Robyn told Luke.

Luke leaned against the door and braced himself, and Robyn broke into a noisy coughing fit as Ralph finally forced the grille free. The thumb bolt turned. Robyn grabbed her brother's legs and pulled with all her strength.

The door jumped open a couple of centimetres, then closed again when Luke put all his strength behind it.

'Hey!' he called. 'Guy sleeping down here. Hold on.'

Dirty, cut and bruised, Ralph wormed his way out into the room and rolled over, panting. Robyn used a cardboard box to block the gaping hole in the wall, just as Abi forced her way inside. She held her Taser in one hand and Robyn's phone in the other.

'What's going on?' Abi said, looking suspicious as hell.

'Not a lot,' Robyn said. 'Can't you get us all couches?'

'This isn't a hotel,' Abi said. 'It's Death Row.' She held the phone out to Luke. 'This has been charged enough. Work your wonders, and maybe Mr Gerhard will change his mind about what's coming next.'

Luke took the phone and stared at it miserably.

'Let me,' said Ralph. 'Try that trick you taught me – you know, where you toggle the standby button with the volume controls in sequence . . .'

'Huh? Oh, yeah. Right.' Luke nodded uncertainly and passed the phone to Ralph.

'Ralph?' Robyn said uncertainly. 'What are you doing?'

'What I have to,' Ralph told her. 'There!' He gave the phone back to Luke. 'You're the expert, Luke. Will it work now?'

'Give me that.' Abi grabbed the phone and stared doubtfully at the home screen. 'It's open. Wasn't that kind of easy?'

Ralph shook his head. 'It's only easy when you know how.'

'Now, please,' said Luke. 'Please tell Mr Gerhard we're sorry and ask him to let us go.'

But Abi had turned away. She closed the door behind her and bolted it without another word.

'What did you do?' Robyn stared at Ralph in horror. 'You let her get it! After all I went through, and you just let her have it!'

Luke nodded, looking angry. 'You should've negotiated, bruh! Made a deal for it. Once she gets the footage, no one will care what happens to us.'

'It's all right,' Ralph told them, sitting on the couch and pulling at his bootlaces, exhausted. 'She won't find the –'

'Of course she will!' Robyn shouted. 'You've handed everything to Gerhard on a plate!'

'They'll find nothing on that phone,' Ralph told her quietly. 'Because that phone isn't yours. It's *mine*.'

Robyn and Luke stared at him as he pulled off his right boot. There, beneath the black fabric of his sock, was a glint of metal.

'So that's why I couldn't unlock my phone,' said Robyn. 'Because it was yours the whole time.'

Ralph reached into his sock and pulled out a phone

151

identical to Robyn's. 'I must've switched our handsets by accident when we ran away from the river. They're both Croc Lodge branded, they look just the same . . .'

Robyn swore under her breath. 'But how did you hide it?'

'I shoved it down my sock when I tried to lead the drones in the wrong direction,' Ralph whispered. 'Didn't want them to see I had a phone in case we could use it to call for help. And the wardens didn't frisk me properly cos they were trying to stop Luke from punching everyone. Good work, Luke.'

Luke smiled for the first time in an age. 'Why didn't you say something sooner, Ralphie?'

'I didn't know it was Robyn's phone until she couldn't open it, even with the sabretooth breathing down her neck,' Ralph explained. 'That's why I made up that excuse for her.'

'I actually believed you,' Robyn said.

'Luckily, so did Gerhard.' Ralph carefully removed the phone from its sweaty hiding place. 'But you two don't realise just how important this thing is – so long as the footage is still there . . .'

Robyn took the phone and tapped her passcode into the handset. This time, of course, it unlocked immediately. She accessed her camera roll and – yes! Over five minutes of recorded video.

'We were so busy staring in shock at the sarcosuchus, we didn't look at the hunters trying to kill it,' Ralph said. 'Zoom in on them now, Rob. Check out the guy in the fancy jacket.'

She did, double-tapping to enlarge the figures in the frame. She hit the pause button then gasped. 'Oh my God.'

'No. No way.' Luke took a step back, as if the video could bite him. 'That's President Mbato!'

'No wonder Gerhard isn't worried about the cops,' Ralph said. 'He owns Mbato. They're working together. They've already got Indah – Stefan's girlfriend – locked up.'

Robyn hugged herself. 'D'you think that was her we saw being marched off when they brought us in?'

'Most likely. And right now they're bringing Dad here – to try to use us against him.'

Quickly, quietly, Ralph told Robyn and Luke the rest of what he'd seen and heard.

'We're screwed,' Luke said simply. 'We're *so* screwed.'

'No,' said Ralph. 'They don't know we have this evidence. If we can get it seen by the right people, it's Mbato and Gerhard who're going down.'

'Do you think the video *has* uploaded to our cloud?' said Robyn.

'Probably not,' said Luke.

Ralph nodded. 'In which case, this phone is the most valuable thing in the world just now.'

Sleep didn't come easy to any of them, but sheer exhaustion saw them crash in the end. Robyn woke to the harsh clatter of the sick-bay door pushing open and several people stomping inside.

Cold dawn light filtered through the window. Ralph got groggily to his feet next to her and Luke stirred on the other side of the room. Shrinker was already in the middle of the room, Abi frowning sullenly beside him, and six more wardens spread out behind them.

'What is this?' Robyn said. 'You must know there's no evidence on the phone you took. You can let us go.'

'We *are* letting you go . . .' Abi said, and Robyn's heart quickened.

'For a toilet break.' Shrinker gave his dead-eyed grin. 'And I'd go if I were you. So you don't crap yourselves later.'

They filed out after Shrinker and Abi. Ralph made eye contact with Robyn but they both knew there were too many guards to try to make a break for it.

While Shrinker pushed Ralph and Luke into the Gents, Abi steered Robyn into an empty room containing a small, basic bathroom, its single tiny window a sealed plate of safety glass. Even though there was no way for Robyn to get out, Abi waited outside the stall.

There's still hope, Robyn told herself. *We've got real footage – footage that can bring down Gerhard's empire and Mbato's career. We just have to get it* seen.

Robyn washed her hands when she came out, and Abi laughed. 'Wouldn't bother. You won't have time to catch anything nasty. Spoiler alert: something nasty's gonna catch *you*.'

Abi forced Robyn ahead of her down a tiled passage to a thick iron door.

'Unbolt it,' Abi said, pulling her handgun from its holster.

The bolts scraped when Robyn slid them across. She heard furtive movement from the other side.

'In,' said Abi.

17

The door squealed open to reveal a large concrete stall. The smell of bleach couldn't disguise a strong animal stink. A woman who looked to be in her thirties and a young man around Luke's age stood together, shifting nervously, in the middle of the room. Another man stood at the far wall, his back to her, beside a large automatic roller-door. Robyn was surprised to see a Q-Base Holosoft logo on the back of his polo shirt.

Robyn recognised the two facing her – they were the unkempt, browbeaten people she'd seen when they were brought to Gerhard's headquarters. The young man's pale, short-sleeved shirt was torn and his dark skin patterned with scrapes and bruises. The woman was glancing anxiously at a locked metal gun locker attached to the wall. There was little else of note in the room apart from some crates in a corner, but a large corkboard had been hung on the opposite wall with photographs of people pinned to it. The tacks had been pushed right through the foreheads.

The young man stepped forward. Robyn watched a hopeful smile flutter on his frightened face.

'Are you . . . are you here to help us?'

'She's here to join you,' Abi said, swaggering through the door. 'Everyone, this is Robyn Ballantyne. Robyn, this is . . .'

'I'm Grant Khumalo, from Pretoria,' the boy said.

'Khumalo,' Robyn echoed. 'Your father isn't Max Khumalo, the Green Freedom Party leader, is he?'

'Guilty as charged,' said Grant.

The GFP was Mbato's main rival; it had been growing in popularity and power over the last few years.

'Dad's always voted for the Green Freedom Party,' Robyn told him.

'That figures,' scoffed Abi.

Grant shrugged. 'Thank you, Robyn.' When the woman and man said nothing, he added, 'This is Indah and Ashwin.'

Robyn started at Indah's name; of course, Ralph had said Indah was a prisoner too, along with Gerhard's other 'nuisances'. She tried a smile but Indah ignored her, taking a step instead towards Abi.

'You must know we're all terrified,' said Indah. 'Tell us what you want and when you're going to let us go. Please,' she added, as if manners might make a difference. From the look of desperation on her face, nothing else had. 'Just let us go home.'

Abi ignored her. 'Were you and Indah trying to get into the gun locker, Khumalo?' she asked in a way that implied she already knew. 'Funny, I didn't think you Green Freedom Party types approved of violence.'

Grant chewed his lip. 'I was only trying to see what was in there.'

'That's more than Mellanby did.' Abi smirked. 'He went out without even trying to take a gun. Didn't end well . . . for him.'

Grant looked across at the photos. Robyn followed his gaze and saw a man she thought she recognised from the news. Or from posters – yes, he was the Green Freedom Party chairman. 'That's Dane Mellanby.'

'My godfather,' Grant said. 'He was always anti-hunting.'

'I would never use a gun either,' Indah said quietly. 'You can't make us.'

'What's this, what's this?' Shrinker pushed Luke and Ralph through the door, then breezed inside. Beardy the ranger and another woman – armed, sour-faced and burly – came in behind him, carrying a laptop and various leads. They started plugging them in to sockets in the wall and loading up some kind of program.

'Ah, young Master Khumalo!' said Shrinker, stepping forward to block Robyn's view. 'And the lovely Indah. I hope our friend Ashwin has been keeping you well entertained as you wait for what's coming.' He grabbed hold of Robyn's arm and propelled her towards Indah. 'Get over there.'

The burly woman shoved Ralph after them and he fell to the floor. Luke crossed quickly to join the others and, with Grant, helped Ralph to stand.

'So, everyone's here. It's time to start this party.' Shrinker smiled. 'Brad?'

Beardy the ranger looked up from the laptop. 'Still uploading the drones' target designations.'

'Network's slow this morning,' said the burly woman.

Leaving Brad tapping at the keyboard she picked up an armful of dark overalls from a crate in a corner of the room and dumped them in the middle of the floor. 'Put these on,' she said. 'There's different sizes to choose from.'

'Just don't take too long about it,' said Shrinker.

Ralph began to struggle into the clothing. Robyn met his eye, and knew his keenness was because he wanted to add an extra layer between prying eyes and his hidden phone.

Grant picked up a pair of overalls. The light caught on several small reflective dots on the fabric as he held it up. He let it fall to the ground.

'Not your size, son?' Shrinker said. 'Just put it on.'

'Why?' said Grant. 'What are you going to do? What did you do to Dane Mellanby?'

'All right.' Shrinker held out a hand. 'Come here, son. I'll show you what we did.'

Confused, Grant tentatively offered his own hand. Shrinker caught hold of it, seized Grant's little finger and twisted hard. Grant's finger snapped, pointing out at an unnatural angle, and he cried out in pain. Shrinker let go and Grant reeled backwards, clutching his hand. Robyn, Ralph and Luke stared at Grant in horror, while Indah turned away. Ashwin didn't react at all.

'That's what we did to Mellanby, son. We broke him!' Shrinker shouted, spit spraying from his mouth as he glared at his prisoners. 'Now, put on the smartsuits. All of you.'

'What are you making us do, Mr Shrinker?' Luke said hoarsely. 'What's gonna happen?'

'You'll see. Now *shift!*'

Slowly, Indah and Luke started to sort through the pile of overalls. Robyn crossed to Grant and checked his hand.

'Your little finger's broken,' she whispered. 'We need to make you a splint.'

'No talk,' said the burly woman. 'Just get on with it.'

Grant mouthed a shaken 'thanks' to Robyn. She picked up one of the smartsuits and held it out to him. With a look at Abi, he took it and, with difficulty, put it on.

'These "smartsuits" stink,' Ralph said.

Robyn realised he was right. The overalls looked laundered and pressed, but stank of something pungent and earthy. 'What is that?'

'Just where they've been stored,' Brad said.

'Bull,' said Ashwin, startling Robyn with his low, gravelly American accent. It went well with his lugubrious face, she decided. 'That smell will help *them* find us.'

Ralph stared at Ashwin as he pulled on the smartsuit. 'Help what find us?'

'The fashion police?' Luke suggested.

Robyn couldn't find it in her heart to smile. Nor could anyone else. She wrinkled her nose as she dressed. Luke zipped up the musky-smelling overalls over his muscular chest.

Abi looked at each of them in turn. Apparently satisfied, she nodded to Brad, who typed a chain of code into the laptop and hit Return. Robyn jerked as a static shock went through her. Ralph and the others jumped too. Indah cried out and Ashwin groaned, though more with fear than in pain, it seemed.

'What did you just do?' Ralph demanded.

'Just something to stop you from taking those things off,' Abi said.

Luke went for the zipper at his neck, but it seemed to have jammed. Robyn tried her own, but with no more success.

'Brad has just switched on electromagnets in the smartsuits,' Abi explained. 'If you try to damage them, the shocks will get progressively more severe.'

Sweating hard, Ashwin went on pulling at his neckline as if trying to tear the suit – and suddenly convulsed. He fell to the ground, groaning even more than before.

'Point proved.' Shrinker's blue eyes were bright and his smile even more smug than usual. 'Another reason not to mess with your smartsuits: they'll help keep you alive. If you're wounded, tech built into the suit compresses the suit to staunch the bleeding.'

'Wounded?' Indah whispered, sounding aghast.

'We're going to have a hunt, boys and girls. And there are rules, so listen closely.' Shrinker nodded to the door through which they'd come. 'Once I've left, the gun locker will unseal and the roller-door will open up. Choose a weapon quickly. You'll have fifteen minutes to get as far from here as you can. And you're gonna want to get away, because –'

'There's an enclosure close by,' Ashwin broke in, 'where Gerhard's latest prehistoric beast experiments are caged up, starving hungry.'

'Ashwin Kingsley,' said Shrinker, tutting like a teacher at a wilful child. 'You didn't have the guts to see your own job through, so now you're trying to steal mine – is that it?'

'Mbato *kills* his political opponents,' Ashwin went on, eyes wide and staring. 'He uses Gerhard's test-tube predasaurs to slaughter us – while they film every second!'

The silence that fell over the room was as thick as the stink from the overalls.

'That isn't funny,' Indah whispered.

'It's not meant to be,' Ashwin said. 'Listen. I worked with your boyfriend. I was Animation Supervisor on *Predasaur* for six months in Pretoria. We thought the beast killings were filmed using actors . . . till Stefan told me the truth.'

'No!' Indah looked at him. 'Stefan couldn't have known about this.'

'He did, and he wanted out,' said Ashwin. 'He tried to make me copy undoctored footage from the digital file vault for him to use as evidence.'

'Tried?' said Shrinker softly.

'I never gave him a thing!' Ashwin protested. 'You know that.'

'Because we stopped you before you could.' Shrinker shook his head. 'And Stefan died before we could stop *him*.'

'From a virus that started here, then mutated,' Ralph piped up. 'You blew up Gauda to try to contain it but it didn't work, did it? It's out in the world. Spreading.'

Indah stared at Shrinker. 'Is that true?'

'Look on the bright side,' said Shrinker. 'Catching the virus won't kill you. It's what's gonna catch *you* that you should worry about.'

Robyn glared at Shrinker, and Indah turned away and started to shake.

'I called up that footage, sure,' Ashwin said. 'But only cos I wanted to prove to myself it wasn't true. So I could sleep at night again.'

'Only, it *was* true,' said Grant, his eyes wide in horror. 'My godfather – all those others, reduced to pictures pinned to a board . . .'

'Target sensors uploaded,' Brad broke in, almost casually. 'Now the drones can tell our "runners" apart. They will be assigned to follow them.'

'Good.' Shrinker clapped his hands and rubbed them in anticipation. 'The scent on the smartsuits attracts the predasaurs. You'll draw every one of them from miles around. That's why you have to keep running, see?'

'These dots on the smartsuits – the drones use them for motion capture,' Ashwin explained. 'The footage is enhanced by animation, the people's faces redrawn, but everything else – it's all really happened. Murder, right there, in front of the cameras.'

'Murder? Nah,' said Shrinker. 'It's just the law of the jungle.'

Robyn looked at her brother, who returned her look helplessly.

'Killed by animals?' Indah was staring in horror. 'Is that what's going to happen to us? You can't!'

'We won't leave this shelter,' Luke said.

'Then you won't find the ammo we've left for you outside,' said Abi. 'The guns in that locker won't be much use to you without live rounds.'

'And there's nowhere to hide in here once that roller-door

opens.' Shrinker lifted his radio. 'OK, we're ready to go. If the big man wants to make his big entrance . . .'

Weighty footsteps sounded outside. Then Julius Mbato strode into sight in a sharp grey suit – he looked smooth as granite and just as hard. It was a surreal moment, seeing the most famous man in the country standing just metres away. Robyn's heart sank. If Mbato had turned up in person to confront them, then there must be no hope of escape for any of them. She thought of the footage on her phone – could she use it to bargain for freedom? No, how could she? Mbato would simply take the handset from Ralph and they'd be back where they started.

'You.' Indah was staring at Mbato. 'You've come to save us?'

'Sorry.' Mbato inclined his head. 'Like any good hunter, I'm simply here to pay the prey my respects.'

'Pay your respects?' Grant almost laughed. 'You want to gloat.'

'Gloat? Oh, no. Didn't your dad ever tell you the folk tale of the leopard and the gazelle?' Mbato stepped closer, his dark eyes boring into Grant's. 'The gazelle has been brought down. She lies wounded and helpless and asks the leopard for pity. The leopard says, "How am I supposed to feel pity for you? That would mean starvation for me."' He smiled. 'You see, Grant, this is nothing personal. It's just the way the equation works between strength and weakness.'

'You're not strong. You're a coward, like any other bully,' Grant said. 'Dane Mellanby taught me that. Rather than earn the approval of the people honestly, you cheat and lie and intimidate others into following you.'

'It's a shame you share the politics of your dad and Mellanby, Grant. Perhaps we could've dealt with you in some other way.' Mbato crossed to the corkboard and pinned more photographs to it – one of Indah, one of Ashwin, one of Grant. 'But with his eldest son and party chairman both taken from him, Khumalo will be much diminished as an enemy.'

'And you scrape through to a third term,' Grant realised.

'I'll march through in triumph,' Mbato said coldly, pinning a picture of Luke to the board. 'Those who stand in my way *do* have a habit of disappearing . . .'

Robyn felt a chill as she saw that the last photo Mbato fixed to the corkboard was of her and Ralph in the sick bay after her ordeal with the sabretooth. *Everyone there on the board*, she thought wildly. *They were brought here, just like us. And then they were killed.*

'Please, Mr President,' Indah protested. 'I've done nothing. Nothing at all!'

'Stefan Jacobs trusted you,' said Mbato. 'We can't take a risk on what he has and hasn't told you.'

'But I'm no risk,' Luke said desperately. 'I don't know anything, I never did a thing –'

'Yet bad things happen anyway. I'm sorry.' With that the president turned to leave the room. 'Set them free, Mr Shrinker.'

Robyn jumped as the metal roller-door began to rumble upwards. The early-morning sunlight streamed into the room. A buzzing outside wasn't made by insects; a cloud of drones hovered in the air. There was something almost gleeful about the way they bobbed up and down, as if in anticipation. Sick with fear, Robyn felt tears prick the back of her eyes, but she managed to keep them at bay. Indah and Luke were less successful.

There was a loud clang behind them as the door to the inner compound swung shut and heavy bolts slid into place. Mbato, Shrinker and the rest had gone.

Luke ran to the door and pulled desperately on the handle, but it didn't budge. 'Please! Open up, come on!'

His voice was drowned by a siren that sounded sharply from the ceiling. It wasn't an alarm, but a signal. It screamed: *Run, prey! As far and as fast as you can. The hunt is about to begin!*

18

'What do we do?' Luke looked at Robyn as the siren faded away. 'What the hell do we do?'

'There's only one thing we can do,' said Ralph. 'We have to play this sick game . . .'

'And win it,' Grant said.

Robyn whispered, 'Ralph, you still have the phone in your boot?'

He nodded. 'If we can get out of this park, we can still beat Gerhard *and* Mbato.'

'I guess we're all going to need a weapon.' Grant crossed to the gun locker and tried to open it with his good hand. The metal door didn't move. For a horrible moment Ralph imagined that there *were* no guns – that this was one more sick joke being played on them. Then a magnetic lock was released remotely and the locker door swung open.

'We should just run,' said Ashwin.

'No,' said Ralph. 'Grant's right – we have to be able to defend ourselves.'

'You defend yourselves.' Ashwin shook his head and ran out into the sunlight. 'I can't fight those things. No one can!'

Ralph watched him run down the track until he was out of sight. One of the drones drifted away after him. Feeling sick, Ralph turned away, looked at the gun locker and forced himself to take stock of the situation. There was a fair selection of rifles, both single-shots and repeaters, as well as handguns. But there were no shooting sticks to help with aiming, and no scopes.

Because we're not the ones doing the hunting, Ralph reflected grimly. *We're the hunted.*

'Anyone here used a gun before?' Ralph asked.

'Yes,' said Grant. 'If you're Ralph Ballantyne, I think we've competed in the same target-shooting tournaments.'

'I'm sorry, I don't remember you,' said Ralph.

Grant smiled ruefully. 'I only remember you because you always won them.'

'I . . .' Indah swallowed, cleared her throat. 'I've been clay pigeon shooting.'

Luke shook his head helplessly. 'Just tell me which of these guns is biggest and best and I'll try to handle it.'

'It depends on the situation,' Ralph argued, 'and on what ammo we've got.'

'Ralph's right,' Grant said. 'We'll take all the guns and check the ammo situation. Then we can choose who takes what. Try and cover as many eventualities as we can.' He looked at Robyn. 'Make sense?'

'Yes,' she said.

'Whatever,' Luke muttered.

What do I choose? Ralph tried to breathe deeply, stay calm. *Lives are on the line here.*

'Come on,' Robyn said, taking guns from the locker and passing them around. Grant took a rifle. Luke took two more and a BFR .44 Magnum. The smartsuits had no pockets, so he held the three weapons in a bundle.

Ralph passed an FA83 – a small revolver – to Indah, though he feared the recoil would throw off her aim. She took it doubtfully. Ralph took a Mauser 98 Magnum, a popular hunter's rifle for delivering a single killing shot from a safe distance. Although he had a feeling that distance from the target was not something they would be able to enjoy.

'Let's move out,' Robyn said, taking two rifles herself. 'Find the ammo so we're prepared, then work out what to do next.'

Grant nodded. 'Yes. Let's move as quickly as we can.'

Luke was first out, but he held back as one of the drones bobbed closer. Grant stepped past him and Luke followed him along the track, the same way Ashwin had gone. Ralph and Robyn followed close behind with Indah.

'Should we run?' said Ralph.

'We might run straight into something that isn't pleased to see us,' Robyn said.

'I'll scout the way ahead,' Grant offered.

The heat was already stealing into the day, the brightness hurting Ralph's eyes. He scanned the mopane and acacia bushes that lined the track, alert to any danger, while knowing he had no way to combat it if it pounced.

'I'm so sorry about Stefan,' Robyn told Indah. 'You got a call from someone a couple of days ago, didn't you? Asking questions about him?'

'Yes. A woman.' Indah looked at her, suspicious. 'Not long after, I was marched away by two thugs from Mbato's security team and brought here.'

'It's not Niko's fault that that happened,' Ralph protested.

'Niko is a doctor – a . . . friend of our dad's. She's the one who rang you,' Robyn said. 'She and I helped to treat Stefan when he was sick. Before he . . . you know.'

'He's better off than us.' Indah shook her head, tears welling in her eyes. 'I never dreamed that Stefan was mixed up in anything bad. I mean, he's a lead animator for video games. How can this have happened?'

Ralph looked at Robyn. 'He tried to do something about it in the end. Like Ashwin. Tried to make it stop.'

'Too late,' said Luke bitterly.

As they reached a bend in the path, they saw Grant running back to meet them. 'Up ahead,' he said, sprinting away again. 'Ammo!'

Ralph and Robyn took off after him as fast as they could. Ralph's body still ached from his ordeal over the last twenty-four hours, but he didn't say a word; he knew that Robyn must be hurting too, but she was hiding it well. Luke seemed too scared to moan. Above them the drones buzzed and whirred as they shot the action through cold camera eyes.

A folding table had been set up at the side of the trail, the sort you might find at a summer fete, laden with cakes. Only this one was weighed down with boxes of ammo and cartridge belts. Ralph scanned the options available: .44 Magnum, .480 Ruger, .475 Linebaugh . . . Of course, the choice of bullet was also critical. Ralph noted that the majority were non-expanding, hard, cast lead or monolithic copper bullets, designed to break through bone and flesh, to stop the heart of the most dangerous game.

'More ammo than I was expecting.' Grant loaded his revolver, wincing from the pain in his broken finger. 'I didn't think Mbato would give us a fighting chance of actually taking down what's coming after us.'

'Maybe it's a trick,' said Luke. 'Gerhard wouldn't want his home-grown monsters killed by us.'

'He doesn't care about any kind of life,' said Robyn, loading Indah's gun for her. 'His breeding or cloning programme – or whatever it is – is well under way. Kill one, he'll grow another.'

'Besides, the more guns there are, the better the ammo, and the longer we stay alive,' Ralph said. 'Gerhard doesn't want the action to be over too quickly.'

'Is that why he's given us this head start?' said Luke slowly.

Robyn nodded. 'The longer we last, the more footage he gets for his game.'

'Sorry, could you all be quiet a minute?' Grant said. 'I think we need to get to grips with these weapons, try them out.'

'He's right. Practise pulling cartridges from your belts and loading up.' Ralph got busy loading his two rifles, glad each had been fitted with a strap for easy carrying.

'I guess I should go practise too,' said Indah, with an almost eerie calm. She turned and walked away, pushing through the vegetation that lined the path.

'Don't go far,' Robyn told her. 'We need to get going as fast as we can.'

Indah didn't answer.

Grant looked at Ralph and Robyn. 'So, how did you get caught up in this? Is it true your dad used to serve with Mbato in the military?'

'Yeah. And he's not a fan,' said Ralph. 'But we're actually here because of Gerhard.'

'We sneaked onto his land and filmed evidence of Mbato hunting for trophy shots,' Robyn added.

Grant's eyes widened. 'My dad heard whispers about that. That's why Dane came out here – to get evidence. The Green Freedom Party can't be seen to be doing anything shady, so he was trying to stay under the radar. Guess Mbato got wind of it.' He shook his head. 'Dane was always there for me. He was more of a father to me than my own dad.'

'I'm sorry.' Robyn put a hand on his arm. 'But Mbato acting like this shows that he's vulnerable. He knows that a scandal would wreck his chances of a third term.' She glanced at Ralph. 'And something might still come up that'll bring him down.'

'Let's hope so.' Ralph shook his head a fraction, hoping Robyn would get the message to keep the phone's existence to herself. For now, anyway. He pushed the loaded gun into Luke's hand. 'Here. Grip it firmly.'

'The only firing I ever did was with a controller,' Luke said. 'What do I do?'

'You have five rounds. Cock the hammer, then fire.' He showed Luke how to swing open the cylinder and use the extractor rod. 'Press this and all fired rounds will be pushed free at the same time so you can reload. Try to lean into the gun as you fire. Don't fight the recoil.'

'All right, all right.' Luke put on the bullet belt and pushed cartridges into the leather loops. 'Why did I ever agree to help you get in here?'

A gunshot cracked out from the bush. Instinctively, Ralph dropped to the ground and rolled under the ammo table for cover. Robyn, Grant and Luke scrambled to follow his lead.

'Indah?' Robyn called. 'Was that you? Are you OK?'

There was silence. Then the crash of footsteps through the undergrowth. Ralph cocked his gun, ready to fire at whatever came out at them.

It was Ashwin Kingsley. His dark eyes were wide with shock.

A drone passed lazily overhead. It dropped something as it went, something that struck the earth like a stone.

It was Indah's revolver. Ralph opened it and checked the rounds. One had been fired.

'She's dead,' Ashwin whispered as the drone buzzed away in the direction of the building they'd run from. 'I was hiding, saw her take the gun . . . saw her put the barrel to her head.' He shrugged, looking stunned. 'She just pulled the trigger. It all happened so fast.'

Robyn looked sick. 'She was so upset for Stefan. In shock. She wasn't thinking straight.'

Luke nodded. 'Life is always worth fighting for. Whatever it takes.'

'Always,' Grant agreed.

'Yes.' Ralph took a deep breath and tried to push down his shock and sadness. 'We need to get out of this, somehow, and make these people pay.'

'And get out of here,' said Ashwin. 'We need to tell people what Gerhard drove Indah to do. We need to show them what he wanted to do to *us* . . . and make sure it can never happen again.' Ashwin came over to the ammo table and took Indah's gun from Ralph. 'Now. What does this damn thing take?'

Ralph got up. 'So, you'll join us now?'

'No choice. Not after seeing Indah . . .' Ashwin trailed off, closed his eyes, brought his fist down on the table. 'Screw Gerhard. Screw Mbato. They want us to make a fight of this? We'll give them a damn fight.'

'Yes, we will,' said Ralph, looking at his sister, who nodded.

'We should try to find open ground, right?' said Luke. 'So we can see them coming and get a clear shot.'

Robyn shook her head. 'On open ground the predasaurs can get behind us. We'll be surrounded.'

'How many do you think there'll be?' Grant asked.

'More than enough,' said Ashwin.

'Where do we go, then?' Luke said. 'Somewhere we can set up a barricade. Maybe a cave?'

'But then we're just stuck in a cave,' Robyn said. 'That doesn't get us closer to freedom.'

'All right!' Luke snapped. 'Why don't you come up with something then?!'

'Maybe if we find higher ground, we can spot the best place to go,' Grant suggested.

'Then let's move.' Ashwin was buckling a second bandolier across his torso. It seemed he'd switched from opting out to being the most determined of them all. Ralph tried to get past the shock of losing Indah and connect with his own anger – harness his adrenaline to make him sharper, more focused. His father had taught him the psychology of hunting dangerous game: mental focus and controlling your nerves were vital when it came to a one-on-one battle.

But just what would be coming after them?

Sorry, Dad, Ralph thought. *Looks like there's no keeping me out of this hunt.*

'We'd better run,' said Robyn. 'The predasaurs will be drawn to Indah's body.'

Ralph set off first, and found he was faster than the others. No one said anything, so he led the way through a wall of dense shrubs, which humans could pass through more easily than larger animals with four legs. On the other side, the going got easier as they climbed a gently sloping hillside rich with acacia and bushwillow trees, their leaves shimmering in the increasing heat. The drones spun overhead, a constant reminder of the horror of the group's predicament.

For a moment Ralph almost felt obliged to hold back and let someone else lead. The others were all older than he was. But he reminded himself there was no precedent for what was happening here, just as there hadn't been for Zouga Ballantyne nearly two hundred years ago. *You don't become an Adventurist by keeping anything back.* The Ballantynes had a tradition of fighting fate face-on. Right now, caught up in this nightmare, Ralph was ready to take on fate and spit in its eye. So what if he was the youngest? He was probably the fastest, and maybe the best shot here too.

But would that be enough?

Sweaty and panting for breath as he reached the top of the rise, Ralph heard a siren sound several bleats. The noise was deep and ominous, designed to chill any listeners, and a clear warning for anyone in the area to get the hell to cover, if only they could find it.

Ralph peered across the valley to the river that snaked through the Gerhard and Crocodile Lodge reserves. Maybe that would be the quickest and least dangerous way back home, bypassing the security gates? Provided they could walk along the banks, the crocs weren't too hungry, the hippos weren't bathing, and that wounded sarcosuchus was out of the picture . . .

Even so, he thought, *it's probably our best hope.*

A couple of kilometres away, he could see the pen they'd been held in, the roller-door firmly locked now. Close by was a concrete building, like a bunker, built against the side of a large mound. The bunker's strong metal doors grated open with a menacing song that carried all the way to where Ralph stood. Then there was a hush, as if the world was holding its breath in the sultry heat.

Even from this distance, Ralph could see that the doors opened onto a wide tunnel that dipped downwards. Seconds later, a pack of snarling four-legged creatures surged out of the tunnel. There were at least fifteen. Ralph felt his jaw drop. The beasts were huge; he guessed they would come up to his chest, even on all fours. Each of the animals had thick, dark-spotted fur. They howled and grunted, swinging their huge misshapen heads from side to side.

Robyn stepped backwards and bumped into Luke. 'Oh my God.'

'Looks like they're trying to catch our scent,' Grant breathed.

'It's the cave hyenas,' said Ralph. 'Beasts out of hell from ten thousand years ago.' He remembered Abi's words on the guided tour: *Big enough to drag their kills to their lair.* But with this many attacking them, there'd be no meat left to save for later.

Ashwin got it too. He swallowed, and it sounded like he was gulping down a brick. 'Once those things catch up with us, they'll tear us apart.'

19

'Come on,' Robyn told the others. While they'd been staring at the snapping hyena-beasts that would soon be chasing them down, she'd quickly climbed the slope to its crest. The ground fell away gradually, and there was thick, tall grass ahead and a dense line of trees that signalled the river.

'What d'you reckon?' Ralph asked, rushing to join her.

'Let's cross the river down there. Might give us some more time.' Robyn glanced back as she spoke. She could hear the cave hyenas' whooping, giggling calls but couldn't see them. 'Where are those things headed?'

'From the flight path of the drones down there, into the forest,' Grant told her. 'I think they were . . . sniffing out Indah's body.'

Robyn's stomach turned. 'It's easier to take a meal that's not going to fight back.'

'Well, we *are* fighting back,' Ralph said firmly. 'Let's go find the river.'

Ralph and Robyn led the charge down the slope. The sound of the hyenas faded.

'Who can handle a gun, then?' Ashwin demanded. 'I went on a self-defence course once, years ago . . .'

'Ralph and I have experience target shooting,' Grant said.

'Your dad leads the Green Freedom Party, though,' said Ralph. 'Aren't they super against guns and hunting?'

Grant looked at him and cocked an eyebrow. 'You never did anything to tick off your dad?'

'I can shoot too,' Robyn told Ashwin. 'I'm not as good as Ralph, though. And there's a big difference between shooting on ranges and facing down a charging animal.'

'Specially when it's an animal from ten million years BC, huh?' Luke spat as he ran, panting for breath. 'Did you see the size of those things?'

Despite the heat, Robyn shivered. *How many cave hyenas will fight over Indah?* she wondered. And how many more would charge straight on in the hope of reaching the fugitive group that smelled just as delicious as Indah did?

'If one of those things comes near me, I'm emptying this whole gun into its jaws,' Luke said.

'We only have limited ammo,' said Ashwin.

'Yes,' said Grant. 'Each shot has to count.'

Ralph was first to reach the sandy riverbank. The river was wide, with dark water and a strong current. Ashwin was about to charge into the water, but Ralph held him back. 'We need to find a better crossing point so we can get over safely,' he said.

'Safely?' Ashwin scoffed. 'Here?'

'A place where the river narrows,' Robyn said. 'The less time we spend in the water, the better.'

'I don't see anything dangerous,' Grant reported.

Robyn saw Ralph raise his left foot, looking worried.

'Phone in water,' he mouthed to her with a grimace.

'Waterproof to forty metres,' she mouthed back. At least that was what the brochure had said. She prayed the phone was as watertight as the guarantee had claimed.

'Come on, then,' said Luke grimly.

'Let's stay on the bank as much as we can,' said Grant. 'In case we need to make a quick swim-away.'

Ralph led the way through the reeds and sandy soil, splashing through the shallows. Robyn caught up easily, a sure sign he was starting to tire. Grant kept up the pace just behind her, with Luke and Ashwin lagging behind.

'Hey,' Ralph said suddenly. 'Where have the drones gone?'

Robyn looked up. There were only three drones hovering over them.

'The others must've been directed away,' Ashwin explained. 'They come with scent capsules. Means they can lead or distract the beasts on the hunt, stretch out the action – bring them to a setting Gerhard thinks will work best in the *Predasaur* game.'

'So Mbato and Gerhard are really watching, then,' Ralph said.

'Course they are,' said Ashwin.

'But that's good.' Luke brightened. 'That means they could still stop this.'

'Maybe,' said Grant. 'But why the hell would they?'

In his viewing suite, Gerhard smiled. He stirred his morning cocktail, happily anticipating his breakfast of eggs Benedict.

He sat on an elegant leather couch in front of a wall of 3D virtual display screens with retinal control. By blinking through his smart-glasses he could make any one of the smaller screens go supersized, filling the wall with high-def images. And just now the drones were leaving him spoiled for choice. One screen showed his hyenas devouring Indah's body (a shame to have wasted a smartsuit on so poor a performance). Another showed more of the pack sniffing and snapping their way up a sloping hillside in pursuit of their prey, while three more screens showed the survivors making their way along the river.

Mbato stood in the corner of the suite, talking on his phone in a clipped monotone. 'Keep me informed,' he told his aide then killed the call, striding over to survey the cave hyenas on Gerhard's screens. 'I should get back to town. More and more incidences of this "plague" are being reported. The opposition is calling for a lockdown. I must be visible to the people.'

Gerhard sipped his Manhattan. 'Visible doing nothing? Not very dynamic with the elections so close.'

'It's your fault that the virus got out,' Mbato snarled. 'I must be seen to stamp it out before it can tear through the country – or the world. Make me the people's saviour and I will sweep the elections.'

'A cure will be found,' Gerhard assured him. 'And then you'll grant me the tech concessions I seek. Even the more . . . controversial ones.'

'It will become law for all South African tech firms to use chips designed by Gerhard Industries,' said Mbato solemnly.

'Chips loaded with spyware that will give you access to the computer systems of all your competitors.'

'What better way to crush my competitors,' said Gerhard, 'than from the inside?'

'*If* you get me that third term,' Mbato said heavily.

Gerhard affected not to hear him. He pulled up another one of the virtual screens, the one showing Luke. 'You know, perhaps I was hasty sending the Van Rok boy out to die with the rest. VanRok Security is probably the only outfit that might detect the malware in our computer chips. It would be useful to have a hold over them.'

'You mean, you save the boy?' said Mbato. 'Demand a ransom for his return, for Van Rok turning a blind eye?'

'It's a possibility,' Gerhard agreed. 'Then again, I can always throw the boy's remains at Van Rok's feet and tell him his wife will be next unless he rolls over and lets me win.' He took another mouthful of creamy poached egg. 'Which would be the most satisfying, do you think?'

Mbato said nothing, silently watching the prey's progress on the screens. The hyena pack was on their trail, drawing closer. Another drone scanned the river ahead of the fugitives, and something there caught Gerhard's attention.

'Oh, perfect.' He took a bigger swig from his cocktail. '*This* is going to be good.'

20

Ralph waded on through the cold river. The noise of wildlife that was usually so relaxing to his ears – fish eagles, hornbills, bottle bills, and all the rustles and calls that filled the bushveld – now chafed at his senses. The din meant they would never hear the hyenas approach. Not that they could do much if they *did* hear them, he supposed. Could they outswim the beasts? He thought of the creatures' muscular hind legs and guessed the answer.

'Can't we get back on land?' Ashwin called as they neared a bend in the river. 'Wading through water's slow going.'

'Look.' Ralph pointed excitedly to where the river narrowed and a cluster of smooth rocks punctuated the flow of water. 'It's safer to cross here.'

'Will the guns and ammo be all right getting wet?' Luke wondered.

'If it's not too deep and we hold as much as possible over our heads –'

'No, wait.' Robyn pointed. 'They're not rocks.'

Ralph looked. One of the rocks had changed into a broad, grey back rising from the black water near the far bank, perhaps fifty metres away. A smooth grey head quickly followed. 'Hippo,' he breathed.

The hippopotamus emerged from the water – a mother standing over five feet tall and weighing over a tonne. A calf straggled after it.

'Who cares about hippos?' said Luke. 'They don't eat meat, do they?'

'Not often.' Ralph shook his head. 'But hippos are super-territorial and quick to attack – especially when they're with their young. They kill more people each year than lions do.'

'I've seen the documentaries,' Grant agreed with a shudder. 'So, do we try to sneak past them? We could move slowly?'

'Slowly?' Ashwin hissed. 'There are monsters on our trail!'

'Hey!' Robyn called out to the hippo, clapping her hands. 'Hey, you!'

'What the hell are you doing?' Luke hissed as the hippo lowered its head, unimpressed.

'It's better to let her know we're here,' Robyn told him. 'Otherwise she might think we're trying to creep up to attack her.'

'Hippos can stay underwater for over five minutes,' Ralph added. 'We don't want one coming up beside us –'

He broke off as another hippo rose into sight not thirty metres away. Another was watching from the shallows on the far side. Luke started splashing his hands in the water, trying to warn it away.

'I wouldn't,' Robyn told him. 'Hippos might stand back but crocs are attracted to splashing. They'll have your hand off.'

'We can't win,' Luke muttered.

'And we can't stay here,' Grant pointed out.

'We need to cross,' Ralph agreed. 'I'll go ahead and see how deep the river is.'

'I'm tallest,' said Grant. 'Give me your guns and ammo. I'll do my best to hold them out of the water.'

'And what if you step on a hippo and get yourself killed?' said Ashwin. 'Then none of us has any weapons.'

'All of you cross,' said Ralph, handing Robyn his revolver and unstrapping his rifle. 'I'll cover you till you've reached the bank. Then you can cover me as I join you.'

'There's no time to argue,' Robyn said. 'We don't have the time to find a better place to cross. I'll take some of the guns and ammo too.'

'I'll keep mine,' Luke announced, slipping off his bandolier.

Ashwin handed his guns and bullet belt to Robyn. Then he struck out for the bank, swimming in a swift crawl. The hippos watched him balefully but didn't move. Grant followed. He caught his broken finger on the bullet belt as he held it above his head and gasped with pain, then set off across the river, taking long strides. The water came up to his chin but he was able to get across. Luke followed, striding clumsily through the water. He stumbled and went under for a few moments. As he recovered his balance, the end of his bullet belt trailed through water.

'Careful!' Ralph shouted.

Soon enough, Luke joined Grant and Ashwin on the far bank. Having secured his own, Ashwin was already fastening Grant's bullet belt for him.

'Go on, Robyn.' Ralph held his rifle at the ready. 'It'll be all right.'

'Hope so,' said Robyn, pointing downriver. Two dark eyes and round ears had broken the surface of the water twenty or so metres away – another hippo, close to the bank.

'Watch out,' Robyn called to Grant, Luke and Ashwin. 'Close company.'

'Drones too,' Ralph noted. All five of the flying camera-bots were buzzing overhead now. He wished he could shoot them down, but could see the armour plating protecting them and knew there was no point.

Robyn had got halfway across the river when the hippo's mouth suddenly yawned open nearly 180 degrees, as if its jaws were hinged. It bared huge, tusk-like canines in an awesome warning. Robyn held still, slowing her breathing, radiating calm. Ralph aimed his rifle at the hippo's head, sweat beading his forehead as he willed the animal to stay put.

The hippo watched Robyn as she took several steps away, then made for the far bank again. Perhaps her weird animal connection trick had worked; the hippo didn't move to stop her. But as she joined the others and Grant helped her out of the water, Ashwin pointed past Ralph's shoulder. 'Oh, God!'

Ralph looked behind him – and saw two giant cave hyenas creeping towards him. For a second he froze in pure horror at the sheer size of them. Someway between wolf and bear, and more savage than either, the hyenas' heads were wide and flattened, their muzzles blunt. Although they looked less deformed than Gerhard's other Ice Age creations, the beasts' eyes were still red and sore-looking. Their muscles bunched and twitched beneath their fur. The largest cave hyena stalked forward, baring rows of razor-sharp teeth in a terrifying grin of anticipation.

For a moment, Ralph felt as if the creature had him under some kind of spell. Then the beast bounded towards him. The drones dived downwards to get a better view. Robyn screamed Ralph's name, jolting him from his shock. In barely more than a second he had cocked the rifle, aimed and fired. The rifle jumped, the recoil pushing it back into his shoulder, but the shot found its mark, ploughing through flesh into the hyena's rib cage. The creature jerked backwards, blood spraying in an arc. The impact sent it into its roaring companion.

Ralph turned and launched himself into the river. To his horror he saw the first hippo they'd seen was powering through the water towards him. Its jaw was wide open, the red pit of its mouth framed with teeth like tusks. Ralph turned onto his back and kicked his legs desperately, trying to keep his rifle out of the water. Shots rang out, bullets peppering the water around him.

'Ashwin, stop!' Robyn shouted. 'You'll hit Ralph!'

As he torpedoed on through the water, Ralph realised that the hippo hadn't been making for him at all. It was heading for the cave hyenas, the largest of which was prodding the dark shallows of the river with one colossal paw. The hyena, after all, posed a bigger threat to the young she guarded so fiercely. Hissing an angry warning at the advancing hippo, three more cave hyenas pushed through the bulrushes, slavering, growling, barking.

Ralph finally reached the far bank. Robyn took his rifle while Ashwin grabbed his arms and pulled him out of the water. Panting, Ralph watched the hippo lunge onto dry land with horrible speed. Its powerful jaws opened and closed just as quickly, chomping into the closest hyena's flank. Howling, the hyena snapped and bit at its attacker's neck – until the enraged hippo tore its attacker in half. Blood splattered the dark water. Then a second mother hippo joined the first to confront the marauding pack. Barking and snapping, a cave hyena circled the new arrival. As the second hippo turned to bellow a warning, another hyena pounced on its back, sharp fangs scissoring. Two more hurled themselves into the fray, filling their jaws with thick grey hide. But the first hippo defended her river mate and yanked one of the hyenas clear: she snapped its backbone and flung the whimpering remains into the path of the pack. One of the cave hyenas bit hungrily into the chest of its helpless pack-brother, and a feeding frenzy began.

Sickened almost as much by the drones bobbing overhead to catch the action as by the primeval bloodshed, Ralph struggled up and took back his rifle. 'Quick,' he gasped. 'Let's move while they're distracted.'

But Luke and Ashwin had clearly got the idea – they were already racing away from the scene, heading up the shallow hill. Robyn and Grant followed, and Ralph hurried after them.

'There'd better be shelter on the other side,' Robyn said. 'Somewhere we can defend, at least.'

Grant nodded. 'If there isn't . . . we're all dead.'

21

Even over the thump of his own heartbeat and the crashing of Robyn, Grant, Ashwin and Luke as they hurtled through the shrubs and grasses, Ralph could hear the cave hyenas getting closer. The beasts' staccato cackles and piercing whoops sent a shiver down his spine.

Ralph overtook Grant and raced into an open area of savannah, where grasses grew thickly in the bright sunlight. As they climbed the hill, the grass gave way to dusty red earth, with widely spaced trees and boulders in the distance.

He heard the whine of a drone. The pack wouldn't be far behind.

'Make for the boulders,' he yelled at the group. They offered a chance of shelter. If nothing else, they'd make a safe wall to put their backs to so they could focus on attacks from the front.

He heard the pack's eerie whoop and call as he ran flat out for the boulders. Robyn and Grant were right behind him, then Luke, but Ashwin was struggling to keep up. The cave hyenas weren't in sight yet, but they were surely getting closer. The most direct path to the boulders meant making their way through a line of young trees with silvery-green flowers bunched among the leaves.

'No!' Robyn shouted. 'They're buffalo thorn. You'll get caught.'

Ralph realised she was right. He swore as he changed direction to run around the trees. They had no time for delays; even seconds could be fatal.

The sound of gunfire behind made Ralph stumble. He looked back. Ashwin had fallen and lay on his side, his rifle raised and smoking. A cave hyena lay nearby, blood oozing from its chest. But the rest of the slavering pack was bounding closer.

'Keep going,' Ralph told his sister. Their eyes met for a second and he saw the anguish in hers, but she led Grant and Luke on to the rocks while he turned and dropped to one knee, swung up his rifle, cocked it and fired in one fluid motion. The hyena jerked onto its hind legs in a grotesque dance, then went down.

Ashwin shot again, but he missed, then screamed as two hyenas descended on him.

Ralph fired. One went down. But the other was pawing at Ashwin's chest, its sharp claws tearing open skin and his smartsuit. If the fabric was supposed to staunch bleeding, it was failing. Mercifully, Ashwin's screams didn't last long. Drones hovered overhead, zooming in for close-ups.

'I'm sorry,' Ralph whispered. 'I couldn't save you . . .'

'Ralph, come on!' Robyn shrieked.

Realising he'd be overwhelmed by the pack if he stayed, Ralph scrambled up. The cave hyenas were fighting among themselves for the best pickings from Ashwin, the more dominant beasts asserting themselves over the smaller wannabes. But, excluded from feeding, the wannabes might try to bring down prey of their own . . .

One cave hyena, rangy and red-eyed, was already eyeing Ralph as he backed away.

Desperately, impulsively, Ralph ran at the buffalo thorn trees. He launched himself into a flying drop kick, splintering the first branches. Each was lined with pairs of barbs, one straight and one hooked. The phone protected part of his ankle but thorns still snagged on fabric and his skin. He felt sharp stings and scratches as he tried to force his way through, panic lending him strength.

All the same, he was barely halfway through the thicket when the rangy hyena ran at him, snarling. Three drones followed; clearly Gerhard didn't want to miss a thing.

'Ralph!' Robyn shouted again. 'Head down!'

Thorns caught in his hair and scalp as Ralph struggled to obey. The crack of gunfire rang out. Splinters of wood exploded close by. But Robyn must have missed, because the hyena was still coming; Ralph heard its exultant, throaty barking as it flung itself into the thicket, snapping wildly at the thorny branches, heedless of the blood staining its fur as it strained to reach Ralph. He had emptied the rifle's magazine so he used it as a club, smashing the stock into the hyena's face. The image of the crazed beast, its red eyes blazing, broken teeth snapping wildly at the rifle jammed in its jaws, burned itself indelibly into Ralph's brain.

Then the roar of a rifle shot went off nearby. The hyena's

body sagged, held up only by the barbs of the thorn tree, which ran crimson. Moments later, another cave hyena was biting into its rump, growling and snapping at competitors for its meal.

Ralph felt a hard grip on his wrist and looked up in panic, but it was only Grant. From the whiff of cordite, he realised that Grant had fired the shot that had saved his life and was trying to haul him free, even with his injured hand.

Ralph fought with renewed strength and with Grant's help tore his way through the rest of the trees. He saw a gash on his wrist – from claw or thorn, he wasn't sure – and felt the sleeve of the smartsuit tighten around it.

'Thanks,' Ralph gasped. 'Robyn, is she . . .'

'She and Luke are finding us someplace to make a stand.' Grant drew his revolver again. 'Come on.'

Ralph's throat burned with thirst, his head was slick with sweat and blood, and his limbs were starting to cramp as he forced himself up the hill towards the boulders. The narrow ridges of the Lebombo Mountains weren't just a distant backdrop; they promised freedom. Then he heard Grant fire the revolver again, and a glance behind confirmed Ralph's worst nightmare. Three more cave hyenas had rounded the buffalo thorn trees and now fanned out to stalk them down. They howled hungrily, unstoppable. Implacable.

True predasaurs, Ralph realised.

The beasts advanced in a line. Grant fired at the hyena to his right, the closest. He missed and swore.

'Give me the gun,' Ralph said.

Grant didn't argue. He passed it to Ralph, who took it, aimed at the closest hyena and fired.

CLICK. The chamber was empty. Out of bullets.

The predasaurs continued their advance.

'Reload!' Ralph cried in a panic. He heard a scuffle of footsteps on the dusty ground and tilted his head back, afraid of attack from behind. But it was just his sister pelting towards him, kicking up clouds of dust. As she ran, Robyn fired off three rounds. Two bullets struck the middle hyena square in the chest, and it went down. The hyenas on either side broke off to feast on their fallen pack-brother.

'Pretty good shooting,' Grant said to Robyn. Ralph hugged her.

'You're welcome.' She gave the briefest of smiles. 'Now, come on.'

Robyn led the way to a natural redoubt, a small space partly enclosed by rock walls on three sides. Luke's rifle leaned up against it; Ralph noticed that the stock was still drying out from the dip in the river. Luke was dragging branches from a fallen buffalo thorn tree towards the entrance to the redoubt, the wood bleached almost silver by the sun.

'You guys OK?' he asked.

'Better than Ashwin,' Grant said sadly.

'Good work with the barrier, Luke,' Ralph noted. 'Should slow them down.'

They helped Luke block the entrance as best they could, wedging the wood tightly between the rocks. 'It might hold them back long enough for us to pick them off,' Ralph said when they were done.

'I'll use my rifle strap to bind the branches,' Grant said.

'But if we block ourselves in, we'll be trapped,' said Robyn.

'Maybe not,' said Luke, hefting his rifle. 'I reckon I can scramble up and out the back. Then I can help you guys climb out too.'

Ralph eyed the near-sheer rise of rock at the back of their little cul-de-sac. He knew he'd struggle to climb it, but Luke was strong and the tallest of all of them; he might just reach the handholds he needed. 'We don't have many options,' Ralph said, opening Grant's revolver. 'I need to reload. Luke, how are you for ammo?'

'I reloaded just now.' Luke picked up his rifle as two of the hyenas advanced towards their shelter, then ran with it to the back of their redoubt. 'I'll get climbing,' he said. 'Maybe I can shoot some of them from above, buy us more time?'

'Do it.' Robyn gave him a smile. 'And thank you.'

The bigger of the two hyenas rushed forward, snarling and snapping at the scanty wooden barricade. Ralph pushed the snub-nosed cartridges into the revolver as quickly as he could while Robyn loaded .270 Winchesters into a Ruger M77. He fired at the cave hyena and struck it in the chest. It yelped and recoiled, whimpering, and its companion stepped closer, a savage growl building in its throat.

'I hate having to kill them,' Robyn said. 'They're only following their instincts.'

'They've been made into monsters,' Ralph declared. 'It's a mercy killing, Rob.'

'I know.' She flicked the safety forward, so the gun was ready to fire. 'I still hate it.'

'Ralph!' Luke snapped, his rifle slung over his shoulder. 'I can't quite make it. Give me a leg up?'

While he helped Luke, Robyn fired a warning shot over the hyena's head. It didn't flinch, but got a firm grip on the barricade and tried to tug it away. The dead branch began to splinter. Grant gripped onto it for dear life, gasping from the pain of his broken finger. 'Shoot it!' he shouted.

'You're in the way!' Robyn ran forward and smashed her rifle stock against the hyena's snout, driving it back.

With Ralph's hands making a stirrup, Luke launched himself up and found a handhold in the ten-foot-high rock face at the rear of the redoubt. Scrabbling for purchase, he swung out his legs and, at full stretch, managed to wedge himself between the two sides of their little fortress. Grunting and panting with effort, he forced himself up and over the lip of the rock face and to safety.

'Yes!' Luke shouted up at the drones, which hummed overhead like metal frisbees. 'Now I can drive off the pack.'

'Wait!' Ralph shouted. 'Help me up first.'

But Luke wasn't listening. Pumped from his success, he took aim at the injured hyena. 'Time to put you out of your misery,' he shouted. He pulled the trigger. Nothing happened. He stared at the barrel. 'Huh? I loaded it OK.' He took aim again.

Suddenly Ralph realised what must have happened. 'Luke, no!' he screamed. 'Don't pull the tr—'

But it was too late. The rifle jumped out of Luke's grip with a fiery blast. Luke screamed and fell backwards, his hands and face burnt, bloody, and peppered with shot. He lay there, shaking.

Grant stared up, wide-eyed. 'What the hell happened?'

'Luke!' Robyn cried.

'His ammo got wet when he crossed the river,' Ralph said, shaken. 'First time he fired, not enough powder charge ignited so the cartridge didn't clear the barrel. He fired the second round with the first blocking it, and . . .'

'Help me!' groaned Luke, writhing in agony.

The predasaurs saw that their prey was distracted and took their opportunity. One of the cave hyenas leaped clear over the barricade, eyes narrowed, jaws wide. Ralph spun around and brought up the revolver as the beast cannoned into him, pinning him to the ground. He fired into the beast's chest and felt its hot blood gush over his body. Robyn and Grant appeared, working together to heave the monster's carcass off him.

Wiping blood from his face, Ralph propped himself up on his elbows. With a splintering smash, the hyenas tore away the barricade. Four more beasts forced their way into the redoubt, hungry for the kill.

22

It's no good, Robyn thought, crouching protectively in front of Ralph and raising her rifle. *There are too many targets. It's the end of the line.*

The cave hyenas lunged closer.

Then six drones dropped down between them and the predasaurs. Electric blue crackles jumped from the drones' metal housings, and the hyenas shook and flinched. Finally, hooting and cackling, they turned tail, driven out of the redoubt.

Grant stared, incredulous. 'What's going on?'

'It's like they were being tasered,' said Robyn.

'But why would Gerhard stop the hunt now?'

Five of the drones drove the hyenas further back to a safe distance. Then Gerhard's voice carried tinnily from the sixth drone. 'I can't let you die just yet,' he crowed. 'This is the best footage I've ever recorded. You'll push sales of *Predasaur* to record-breaking levels!'

Robyn felt despair weigh down her stomach. She didn't want to fight on, pitted against animals like gladiators in an arena, never knowing when the end would come, when the emperor would finally grow bored of them and give a thumbs-down to signal their end.

'Besides,' Gerhard went on, 'your father has been spotted on my land. He must have come downriver to rescue you! I'd hate for you to die without him being able to see it for himself . . . or vice versa.'

Helplessly, Ralph stared at Robyn.

Grant closed his eyes. 'And we thought the biggest monsters were out here.'

I won't give him the satisfaction of rising to his bait, Robyn vowed. 'Gerhard, please – Luke can't fight any more. He needs help!'

'The hyenas will stop his pain,' said Gerhard. 'Soon enough.'

'No, please!' Luke shouted, his back turned to the others, on his knees on the bloodied rock above. 'Save me, and I'll help you. Ralph switched the phones!'

'No, Luke!' Robyn shouted, horrified.

'I'm sorry!' Luke twisted around to face them. His once handsome face was a mess of blood and bruising, and on one side his blond hair had burned away to stubble. 'I'm sorry, I'm not strong like you. I can't do this.'

Gerhard's voice purred from the drone's speakers. 'You have something to say, Luke?'

'Ralph's got the evidence,' Luke yelled. 'Mbato shooting at that prehistoric croc thing while his friends die around him. He's got it.'

Ralph stared up at Luke, his face ashen. Robyn wanted to deny what he'd said, but her throat had dried and she felt sick. Though Luke's betrayal shocked her, she knew that she'd pushed him to this by bringing him out here. Deep down, Robyn wasn't sure she could blame him for selling them out now.

'Please, Gerhard.' Luke sobbed bloody tears. 'Help me.' He was on his feet. Robyn followed his gaze and saw that the cave hyenas were climbing stealthily towards him. 'Keep those things away.'

'Well, Luke, I'm inclined to believe you,' Gerhard said. 'It explains why we couldn't find Ralph's "lost" phone. I'll be sure to have words with the ranger who searched him when he captured you all.'

The drones that had hovered ready to see off the approaching hyenas suddenly took off back into the air.

'Wait!' Luke bellowed. 'Don't just go; you need me! I can open the phone, get the Mbato film back from the data cloud!'

'No Ballantyne will live long enough to use it.' Gerhard's voice grew fainter as the sixth drone sped away too.

Robyn wiped tears from her eyes as Luke scrambled weakly away from the hungry hyenas. One was bigger than the rest, his powerful hind legs propelling him through the air. Luke kept going, and was soon lost from sight. Ralph raised his gun to try to take down the pursuing animal, but it followed Luke.

'Keep away!' she heard Luke yell. 'No!'

The howl of the cave hyena was the only reply. Robyn tried to climb out of the redoubt but Grant held her back, clung on to her. She screamed in frustration and despair.

When her screaming stopped, there was no other sound but the yap and growl of the predasaurs. They were keeping their distance after their tangle with the drones, but were still ranged around the exit from the redoubt, keeping their prey penned inside.

'There's only one way out of this now,' Robyn whispered. 'Isn't there? And Luke just took it.'

Mbato was grim-faced as he turned away from the sight of Luke's fallen body on the screen. 'We can't afford for anything to happen to that phone,' he said. 'I must know what they have on me.'

'We'll sort it.' Gerhard put his landline telephone on speaker and dialled a number. The thrum of the ring tone filled the air. 'I'll have stretcher drones fetch Luke's body back here – we don't want the hyenas distracted picking at him. Meanwhile . . .'

The phone was answered. 'This is Shrinker.'

'Kurt Shrinker, the infamous mercenary, whose handpicked team can't even pat down a teenaged kid?' Gerhard's voice was colder than the ice in his cocktail. 'You missed the boy's phone. Get your team ready. We're paying a visit to our survivors in person.'

Shrinker hesitated. 'I was just getting ready to intercept Ballantyne. Figured that was more important to –'

'Leave the "figuring" to me, Shrinker.' Gerhard paused, surveying his virtual monitors, noting where Ballantyne and Xai were as they ran through his land. 'In any case, it seems to me that if our trespassers continue on this course towards the river, they'll converge on our field of operations.'

'All right,' said Shrinker. 'I'll brief the team. We'll be out in five.'

'Make it three.' Gerhard hung up and sat back down to finish his breakfast as if nothing had happened.

'This is perfect,' Mbato muttered. 'We need to get out there, Gerhard. Experience the end of the entire Ballantyne dynasty . . .'

Gerhard dabbed at his lips with a napkin. 'I prefer to watch it from here in comfort, perfectly captured on the screen.'

'You mean you don't like to get your hands dirty.' Mbato permitted himself a small smile. 'Ballantyne's been elusive prey for so many years – he deserves to die at my hands, not just as footage for your precious game.'

'The game that helps fund your precarious political ambitions,' Gerhard reminded him.

'And don't you get off on it? You love the thought of millions of gamers watching real people dying without knowing it.' Mbato sneered. 'Gives you power over them, doesn't it?'

'They're playing my game,' Gerhard conceded, 'in every sense.' He stood up. 'But perhaps you're right. I will accompany you, with Shrinker and his team. Because I've had a delicious thought about how I can best deal with Ballantyne.'

Mbato held open the door. 'Then, let's go.'

* * *

Robyn sobbed, her determination to keep things together broken by Luke's last moments. She curled up against the rocky side of their shelter, dimly aware of Ralph and Grant pulling the wooden barricade back into position and trying to shift a large rock to reinforce it, providing additional safety. But her tears dried in the end, leaving her head pounding.

'I didn't see it,' Robyn announced.

Ralph looked over at her. 'See what?'

'The hyena that got him. It hasn't come back.' She shrugged. 'Perhaps Luke got away . . . and it's still hunting him.'

'I don't think so, Robyn.' Grant came over, hesitant, and brushed his fingers against her arm. 'Hey. You're bleeding.'

Robyn looked down and saw a tear in the smartsuit, marked with blood from a deep cut in her arm. 'I didn't even notice. Ha. Now it hurts.'

Grant nodded. 'Adrenaline. You were too busy surviving.' He pulled a couple of leaves from his bullet belt – glossy dark green on one side and slightly hairy and paler on the other – and started to fold and crush them between his fingers. 'I grabbed these from the buffalo thorn tree. They soothe wounds.'

Robyn watched as he gently rubbed the sap into her cut. 'Is this what they teach you in the Green Freedom Party?'

'This, and the recipes for some really terrible smoothies,' Grant told her. 'Plan is, first we take power – then we publish our cookbook.'

Robyn ignored him. Her cut tingled, thanks to the leaf

sap. She knew he was only trying to brighten her mood, but she wasn't ready to smile again. Nowhere close. She could hear the cackling yips of the cave hyenas and turned to Ralph. 'Any developments out there?'

'They're still holding back, watching the drones.' The little robots were circling overhead like birds of prey. Ralph stood motionless, his head tilted to one side. 'I thought I heard an engine. Thought it might be the cavalry coming to our rescue. I guess not.' He sighed. 'Sound travels weirdly over terrain like this – it rolls and bounces, fools you into thinking something far away is a lot closer.'

'I wish those damn hyenas were *really* far away.' Robyn took a deep, shuddering breath. She could allow herself to feel grief and anger and other dark, sticky feelings later. There was no time now. 'Now they know about the phone, should we hide it?'

'The drones will be watching,' Grant reminded her.

Ralph nodded. 'Anyway, *when* we escape, we may not have time to come back to get it.'

Robyn forced a smile that tried to match his optimism. 'OK. Then, how are we doing for ammo?'

'We can't risk using any more cartridges that might be damp,' said Ralph. 'Which leaves us well short. I've got six rounds left for the rifle.'

'I've loaded this thing with the last of my ammo,' Grant reported, motioning with his revolver. 'Three shots and I'm out.'

'And I've got just four in the magazine.' Robyn looked at Ralph. 'Thirteen rounds altogether.'

'And easily as many of those things left,' Grant noted.

'We'll need every shot to be a kill.' Ralph looked pale but determined. Even now, Robyn could glimpse the man he would become in a few years – if they survived. He held the rifle as if it was part of him, a precision tool to wield after his endless hours of practice. She was so proud of him; proud to be his sister.

'What if we *do* get past the predasaurs?' Robyn said gently. 'Do you think Gerhard and Mbato will let us walk out of here?'

'If we could only get to the mountains,' Grant said, 'hide out there till it was safe . . .' He looked down at the corpse of the cave hyena beside Robyn. 'Who am I kidding?'

'Wait a sec,' said Ralph. 'Could we prop that thing up against the back rock, use it as a stepping stone, and climb out of here the same way Luke did?'

'If we did, we wouldn't be trapped any more,' Grant agreed.

'Maybe we can get out before the predasaurs attack,' Robyn reasoned. 'Then we wouldn't need to shoot them at all –'

But it was too late. A long, ululating howl from the largest cave hyena was answered by keening calls from the others. Within moments, they had joined the alpha, gathering around him, prowling the crimson ground, pawing up clouds of red dust.

Ralph looked at Robyn. 'Maybe Gerhard will send in his drones again to stop them.'

Robyn shook her head angrily. 'I bet this is the footage

he really wants. He'll show Dad and then dress it up as entertainment for the world . . .'

As if on some unspoken command, the predasaurs flew towards the barricade.

23

As the cave hyenas bounded towards him, Ralph aimed at the closest and squeezed the trigger. But the beast darted nimbly aside and the bullet missed its mark. A second later, Ralph was knocked backwards as the hyena bashed against the barricade, snapping at them. Ralph swung up the rifle and fired again, opening a crimson tear in the animal's barrel chest. The other beasts recoiled quickly, retreating into a ragged line, like they were queuing to get inside – a tactic that made them far harder to hit.

Just how smart had Gerhard's experts made these beasts?

As the line advanced, the hyena in front hissing and spitting its hate, Ralph felt guilt tug at his concentration. This wasn't like culling injured or weak predators on their own reserve. This was savage and bloody and *wrong*. He tried to detach himself, to pretend that he was playing a VR version of *Predasaur*. As the cave hyena in front darted forward, Ralph shot again. This one needed two hits to bring it down, but immediately the next was leapfrogging the corpse, using it as a springboard to dive at Ralph. He shot it in mid-air but had to leap aside as it cleared the barricade. Ralph hit the ground face-first and rolled over.

Two front paws hammered down on his chest. Teeth gleamed in wide-open jaws. Crimson eyes shone hellfire. Ralph tried to move but he was pinned. The claws pushed through his smartsuit. Drool splashed from the hyena's jaws onto Ralph's face.

Then a single gunshot rang out. The predasaur jerked. As the beast rolled away, dead, Ralph saw his sister on top of the rock face above. Smoke wisped from her rifle barrel. She and Grant had made it out! Grant was shooting down at the rest of the cave hyenas; the creatures' attempts at hiding were no use when they were preyed on from above.

'Get up here!' Robyn yelled.

Galvanised by his miraculous survival, Ralph scrambled over to the dead hyena, which had been pushed against the rock as a stepping stone. He saw that Robyn and Grant had wedged an empty rifle between the natural rock walls at 45 degrees, creating a rung he could step onto to propel himself up to the top. Even without ammo, that rifle had saved their lives, no doubt.

Grant and Robyn had set off in the opposite direction from Luke. From here they were able to pick off the pack one by one. Six snarling bodies down – and Ralph quickly made it seven. Finally, screeching in defiance and tearing chunks of flesh from the corpses of their pack-brothers, the others retreated.

'We did it!' Robyn whispered in disbelief.

Ralph pointed at the drones overhead. 'You don't think Gerhard's gonna leave it at that, do you? "Well played, kids, good game – now, get on home?"'

Robyn nodded. 'We need water,' she said. 'I feel sick.'

'Dehydration,' Grant agreed. 'Me too.'

'We have to get to the river,' Ralph said.

Grant's eyes widened. 'After the bloodbath last time? It'll draw every croc for miles.'

'We don't have much choice,' said Ralph. 'Let's stick to the higher ground and find the quickest way down.'

Together, they followed the rocky trail along the ridge. Ralph surveyed the distant mountains and plains: they were a majestic sight. But always the drones cut in on his thoughts, haunting the scene like carrion. The river coiled below them like a vast, glittering python, but the slope was too steep here for them to descend safely. Ralph was looking for a path they could take.

Then he heard a growling from ahead. A cave hyena stalked out from behind a boulder. Blood stained the ragged fur of its chest. Ralph brought up his rifle, cocked it and fired. The hyena ducked behind the rock and didn't come back out. Robyn and Grant had their guns at the ready too. The drones circled nearer for close-ups.

'Where'd it go?' Grant whispered.

Robyn barely had time to see the cave hyena before it pounced from behind the boulder. She went down under its paws – then found herself used as a springboard as the beast made for Ralph and Grant.

Time seemed to slow. Robyn heard the crack of gunfire some way off – who was shooting at them now? No, not *at* them. The next second the beast gave a horrible, frothing howl as a bullet tore into its flank when it was in mid-pounce.

Though it was already dead, its momentum sent its body cannoning into Ralph.

It knocked them both off the ridge.

'Ralph!' Robyn screamed.

Frantically, Ralph twisted in mid-air, trying to keep the hyena's body beneath him as they careened down the slope, red dust streaming out behind them like a comet's tail. Then the hyena's body crunched into a rock and they were separated. Winded, Ralph tried to curl into a ball, tucking in his head, clinging to his rifle. He was choking on dust, unable to check his speed. The world was a confused haze, sky and slope chasing their tails, until suddenly he was in some long grass, rolling over and over as the ground levelled out.

Dimly he heard Robyn calling to him. Through the red, smoky dust he saw her and Grant picking their way carefully down the treacherous slope, the ever-present drones still hanging overhead. The hyena lay in a twisted sprawl further up the slope. Gingerly Ralph flexed his limbs. By some miracle, nothing seemed to be broken. Could the same be said for the phone? He was worried that it had been flung free – but no, it was still wedged against his bruised, tender ankle, where it had rubbed the skin raw.

Ralph staggered down to the riverbank and drank thirstily from the brackish water before washing his hands and face. The river was a couple of metres deep here, the far side studded with stones. Over the water's burble, he thought he could hear something else: a sort of humming sound. He strained to listen, but it was no good.

Wearily, Ralph stood and checked his rifle, waiting for Robyn and Grant to catch up with him. The weapon was dusty but the barrel looked undamaged – that was something, at least.

'Thank God you're all right,' Robyn called as she ran to join him.

'Just about,' Ralph said, placing a hand on their shoulders. 'Thanks for getting the hyena.'

'*We* didn't shoot it,' Robyn told him. 'And we didn't stick around to see who did.'

Grant went down to the river's edge and drank greedily. Robyn joined him and dipped her head in the soothing water.

Then the crackling of tyres over brushwood and the hum of a solar engine broke the peaceful scene. Ralph whirled around to see an open-top truck lurching into sight. *That's what I heard!* he thought.

Shrinker's sick sidekicks, Abi and Brad, were among the six personnel in the back. They were aiming automatic weapons straight at them.

'Don't move!' Abi shouted as the truck lurched to a stop beside the riverbank. 'Drop your gun.'

Ralph looked at Grant and Robyn. They had been caught unawares while trying to refresh themselves, their weapons in the dust where they'd left them. With a stone-heavy heart, Ralph laid down his rifle.

'Is this an intervention, Abi?' Robyn called. 'Did you shoot the hyena? What's wrong? Were we doing too well?'

'Things have changed,' Abi informed her.

Ranger Brad stepped up to Abi's side. 'We're still getting no response from the drones,' he said. 'It's like they're stuck in a holding pattern, just the other side of the ridge. They're showing nothing but the ground.'

Abi pulled a face. 'But Group Two has eyes and Tasers on the predasaurs, right?'

Brad nodded. 'There's no danger of hyena attack here.'

Just then, a Gerhard Reserve truck crested the ridge and half-steered, half-skidded down the slope towards them.

'Mr Gerhard is bringing two late players to join the fun. Should be quite the reunion . . . while it lasts.'

Ralph stared first at her, then at the truck as it rumbled closer. He saw Gerhard at the wheel and Mbato in the passenger seat. Shrinker was in the back holding two men at gunpoint.

Ralph's heart leaped halfway up his throat. 'Dad! Xai!'

'Oh, God, Dad, are you all right?' Robyn yelled.

'Kids!' As the truck braked, Roland tried to stand. But Shrinker cracked him on the side of the head with the butt of his handgun and he fell against Xai, gasping.

'Leave him alone!' Ralph shouted.

Shrinker smirked, then brought the butt of the gun down on the back of Roland's neck for good measure. Roland gasped and slumped forward. Xai glared at Shrinker. Shrinker slapped him on the cheek fondly. 'Don't worry, little guy. I'll give you some attention too, soon, I promise.'

Gerhard, immaculate in a khaki safari suit, got out of the truck. Ralph fixed him with a look of loathing. Mbato got out of the other side and stood looking at Robyn, Ralph and Grant, as if sizing them up. It was surreal, lined up at gunpoint before the country's president.

'Kids,' Roland said hoarsely, raising his head. 'Are you all right?'

'Gerhard's predasaurs have been hunting us down,' Ralph said.

'Predasaurs? We've seen monster beasts in the park –'

'He bred them. They killed Luke,' Robyn broke in, speaking quickly, afraid tears would choke the words before they came out. 'I'm so sorry we came here. I –'

'An apology! So sweet,' said Gerhard. 'And you, Mr Ballantyne, will you apologise for trespassing?'

'You're the one who's going to be sorry for what you've done,' Roland said quietly, sitting back up. 'Killing kids!'

'Where is Niko Haart?' Mbato asked casually.

'She stayed behind at the Lodge,' said Xai.

'Learning more about the virus you've unleashed,' Roland added, looking from Mbato to Gerhard. 'If we don't return safely, SangoMed will release a statement to the press confirming that the virus has spread from an extinct species of animal resurrected by Gerhard with full government backing. That's true, isn't it? And it won't help your chances of a third term, Mr President.'

Mbato scoffed. 'Lies. Smears. I'll sue.'

'And it will be the last story Niko ever tells,' said Gerhard. 'I'll see to that. Once I've seen to you.' He gave a thin-lipped smile. 'Now then, Ralph. Hand over your phone, please.'

'I hid it,' Ralph said. 'I'll only tell you where if you let us go.'

Mbato yawned. 'Take off your boots.'

'Why?' said Ralph.

Mbato glanced at Shrinker. He drew back his fist and punched Xai in the face. Robyn cried out but Xai didn't murmur, even as blood flooded from his nose.

'Take off your boots,' Mbato said again.

'Do it,' Grant told Ralph quietly. 'Before they kill one of us.'

'They'll kill us anyway!' hissed Ralph.

'Grant's right,' said Robyn. 'There's always a chance.' She heard herself say the words, but in truth couldn't see a way out. Dad and Xai were powerless, and there was no way that Gerhard was going to let them walk away. All she could do was stay calm, alert to any advantage they could seize.

God knew, they had nothing to lose.

Ralph crouched down and fumbled with his bootlaces.

'Wait a moment.' Gerhard held up his hands and smiled. 'I think we should recognise that Mr Ballantyne's children have been extremely resourceful here. They found a way into my innermost sanctum, they gathered evidence that would have caused a good many questions to be asked of President Mbato, they've shot and killed a large number of extremely expensive animals . . . and they even lured their father straight into my hands!' He began to clap slowly then looked expectantly at his staff, who joined in with the ragged applause like zombies. 'Yes, I salute your children, Mr Ballantyne. And if you do as I tell you, I will permit you to choose which one of them gets to go on living.'

The clapping trailed off. Robyn felt a shiver run through her. Grant put a protective arm around her. Ralph just stared.

Roland looked hatefully at Gerhard. 'What did you say?'

'I'm offering you the chance to leave here with one of your children still breathing.' Gerhard smiled wanly. 'I can't let them both live, I'm afraid. They really have wasted too much of my valuable time. But surely it's better to do as I ask and live on with one of them than for you all to die together?'

'Don't listen to him, Dad!' Robyn shouted.

'Well, now, Gerhard.' Roland went on staring. 'What exactly do you want from me?'

'You've been a thorn in my side for years, and your feud with our great president here has endured for far longer. So here's where you can turn things around.' Gerhard smiled and leaned against the open door of his truck. 'What we require from you is this: you announce your support for President Mbato's third term.'

'No way,' Ralph said automatically.

'You give me your unequivocal endorsement, Ballantyne,' Mbato went on. 'Your voice carries weight in the conservation community. You'll say that you were wrong to criticise trophy hunting.'

'Dad, you can't!' Robyn cried.

'And when Mbato announces that trading in ivory will resume, you will shout down the protests from the Green Freedom Party and the rest of the moaning minnies,' Gerhard added. 'Don't fret, it'll be my ivory we trade in – grown from my experimental animals.'

'You're mad, both of you,' said Roland. 'Mbato, have you not noticed there's a new epidemic spreading across South

214

Africa – and it started here? Hundreds of thousands could die. Forget your schemes for once, man. You're meant to be a leader – this has got to be your priority!'

Mbato made no response.

'I'm glad you're considering priorities, Mr Ballantyne,' said Gerhard. 'You have it in your gift to save one of your children. Let's see which you love the most.'

'You sick . . .' Roland shook his head. 'You can't be serious.'

'You know, several people have said that to me recently. They quite quickly learn that, actually, yes. I can.' He nodded to Shrinker, who climbed down from the truck and pulled out a Glock pistol. Roland started forward, but Abi pointed her rifle at Xai's neck.

'I wouldn't move,' Mbato said. 'Or your faithful little rogue takes the bullet he should have received on our final mission together.'

Shrinker came over and stood behind Ralph and Robyn. He aimed the Glock at the back of Ralph's head, then swung the gun around to point at Robyn's instead.

'Decisions, decisions,' Gerhard said.

Robyn was revolted by how much Gerhard was loving this; it was as if he'd grown in height, demonstrating the power he had over all present. She looked helplessly at her dad, who was staring at Ralph and Robyn as if trying to lock every detail about them to his memory. The choice was horrible. Impossible. Perhaps if she lunged at Shrinker now – took him down, raked her nails over his face – Gerhard would have her shot and Dad would take Ralph out of here. She tried to push away her fear, to summon the courage to make the choice she knew her dad could never make.

She felt the barrel of Shrinker's gun press against the back of her neck.

Ralph watched helplessly as the smirking Shrinker pressed the barrel of his gun into Robyn's neck. He bunched his fists, summoning the courage to run at Gerhard and punch him as hard as Shrinker had punched Xai. And if he was shot for it – well, at least the decision would be made and these maniacs might let Robyn live. If he didn't do something, then maybe all of them would be –

Suddenly there was an eruption from the river behind them.

A monstrous dark grey shape surged up and over the bank: a huge crocodilian beast with a head the size of a sofa. Its jaws were the length of a man, and its mouth was open wide.

Sarcosuchus, Ralph realised. Wounded but still very much alive, attracted by the stench of blood and bodies in the river – and craving kills of its own.

Shrinker fired the Glock into the jaws of the predasaur. Its fangs shattered but the sarcosuchus didn't break pace. It turned its head to one side, its jaws gaping, then clamped its jaws shut around Shrinker's chest. He gave a scream that died quickly into liquid gasps as the monster's teeth scissored through his flesh.

'Kill it!' Mbato bellowed.

Ralph grabbed Robyn and dived to the ground beside

Grant as Abi and the rest obeyed their president. Automatic weapons rattled their death song. But the bulk of the bullets hit Shrinker's flailing body, riddling him with holes until a second massive bite from the sarcosuchus tore him messily in half. His legs flopped to the ground.

Ralph wriggled backwards on his elbows, trying to reach his rifle. Gerhard got up and ran for his truck. Mbato was leaning over the bonnet, firing round after round at the sarcosuchus. But Shrinker's body-armoured torso was still clamped in its jaws, helping to protect its vulnerable head. The beast turned and swept its huge tail around. Their legs knocked from under them, two of Gerhard's guards were sent flying like bails from a broken wicket. One of them smashed into Abi, who was reloading her gun. She fell to the ground. Beside her, Ranger Brad tried to drag her clear of the monster, only to stray too close to those giant jaws. His rifle, then his arm vanished down the sarcosuchus's throat. Screaming, he fell backwards on top of Abi and the monster trampled them both.

Ralph wanted to shut his eyes. His world had become a whirl of death and blood and people screaming. He and Robyn and Grant were safe enough for now, ignored by the sarcosuchus, but he needed to know that his dad and Xai were all right too. He saw them jump from the truck, its bulk a barrier between them and the giant predasaur.

But now Mbato had seen them too. He shifted his aim to cover Roland, his teeth bared in a savage grin. 'No escape this time,' he said.

The next second, a jeep came flying into sight over the

ridge. It bounced crazily down the slope towards them, making straight for Mbato. Through the windscreen Ralph saw who was driving.

'No way,' he breathed. 'Niko?'

There was no time for Mbato to take a shot at her. He scrambled into the truck and slammed the door closed. Roland and Xai scattered. Gerhard clawed at the wheel and the truck leaped forward.

Too late.

Niko's yell of defiance rose over the hum of the electric engine as she sent the jeep smashing into Gerhard's truck. The force of the impact crushed the front of the jeep and threw the truck over onto its side. The heavy vehicle landed on the sarcosuchus, which gave a gut-wrenching roar.

'Niko!' Roland shouted. Straight away, he and Xai were running for the jeep.

'Come on.' Robyn pulled Ralph and Grant to their feet. 'We need to help them.'

'Wait!' Grant pointed. The injured sarcosuchus had got to its feet and dragged its bloodied bulk clear of the wrecked truck. Now it lurched towards Roland and Xai.

'Look out!' Robyn screamed.

Ralph snatched up his battered rifle, already reacting, already taking aim. He knew that if he wanted to take it down, he'd have to hit its brain or its spinal cord. Anything else, even a millimetre out, would still let the animal move – and attack. The thoughts flashed through his mind and fled as Ralph forced himself to be calm.

He took control.

Took a breath.

Took the shot.

The gun fired. The sarcosuchus reared into the air, half-rolling, then fell flat and didn't move.

He'd done it. The perfect anchoring shot.

Ralph took a deep gasping breath and turned his head to see Mbato, trying to climb out of the upturned truck's broken window, staring at him with hatred. He realised that was the killing shot that Mbato had bungled, the failure they'd caught on the video. He had bested Mbato in the most painful way possible: cheating him of the hunter's perfect kill.

Mbato raised his gun, aiming at Ralph. Ralph froze. He was out of ammo, and there was no time to reload. But Grant had his back. He fired the revolver and hit Mbato in the left forearm. Mbato cried out with pain.

'Now don't move, Mr President,' yelled Grant. 'Or I'll kill you like you killed Dane Mellanby.'

Mbato clamped his right hand over the wound in his arm. 'Gerhard!' he called. 'Gerhard, wake up, dammit.'

In the cab, Gerhard groaned. He was sprawled against the steering wheel.

'I'll keep an eye on the bad guys,' Grant told Ralph and Robyn with a weary smile. 'Go.'

Roland had helped Niko from the mangled jeep and she sat in the grass, rubbing her neck, seeming in a daze. He looked at Ralph and Robyn and beamed as they ran towards him. 'Ahhh. Children, incoming!'

'Dad!' Ralph said, bundling into his father's arms. Robyn threw her arms around them both and Xai piled in too.

'So much for Niko staying at Crocodile Lodge,' Robyn said.

'A lie,' Xai agreed. 'We took the cabin cruiser into Gerhard's land. When we deployed, we left Niko on board in a camouflaged jeep. She drifted further downriver . . .'

'And since you're transmitting a homing signal, I could follow your progress,' Niko said woozily. 'When you stopped moving for a while, I realised you must have been captured.'

'And you knew Gerhard would take Dad and Xai straight to us so he could gloat,' Ralph reasoned. 'So you knew just where to find us.'

'And come to the rescue,' Roland said proudly.

Robyn's smile congealed. She wanted to tell her dad everything that she and Ralph had been through – to see the pride in his eyes for her, not for Niko. But then, if it hadn't been for her unexpected arrival . . .

'Thanks, Niko,' Robyn said.

Niko smiled up at her, surprised. 'I make an unlikely cavalry, I guess,' she admitted. 'But it worked, huh?'

'Thank God the drone-jammer I stowed in the jeep worked and stopped you from being spotted from the air,' said Xai. 'I could only guess what frequencies they'd operate on.'

'Tut, tut,' said Ralph. 'I thought the family motto was "Who prepares, wins"?'

'Prepare for a hug,' Niko said, and put an arm around him. She reached out to Robyn too. But then the low whine of an engine signalled the arrival of another truck. Mbato stayed silent, but he smiled grimly.

'Abi said something about Group Two,' Grant remembered. 'They must have come for Gerhard.'

'Take cover,' Roland barked. He and Xai helped Ralph, Robyn and Niko to hide behind the wreck of the jeep. Ralph reloaded his rifle and passed it to his father, who fired at the approaching truck, shattering its windscreen. It skidded to a halt. Someone in the truck returned fire with a semiautomatic, and bullets pinged and ricocheted off the jeep's twisted carcass.

'Grant?' Robyn shouted, staring about wildly.

He waved to her from his cover in the rushes on the bank.

'Come on, man!' Mbato dragged Gerhard out from behind the wheel. The truck parked beside the overturned vehicle, using it as a shield from further Ballantyne bullets. Mbato pulled Gerhard onto the new truck, then it roared away, Mbato firing wildly as it went.

His face grim, Roland rose from behind the jeep. 'They'll be back in numbers,' he said.

'And any cave hyenas left will be drawn to the dead here,' Ralph said. 'This place is gonna get seriously unfriendly.'

'Unfriendlier than you can imagine,' said Grant, pointing to the riverbank. Dark, beady eyes stared at them from the shallows – regular crocodiles, but no less dangerous or frightening for it. Slowly, cautiously, they began to slither up the bank.

'This is Grant Khumalo, Dad,' Ralph explained quickly. 'Son of –'

'Max Khumalo.' Roland offered his hand to shake as

221

they got in the truck. 'I know your father. Pleased to have you with us.'

'I'd better check the other truck,' Xai told Roland. 'With luck, we can use it to get the hell out of here.'

'And go home?' Niko asked.

'I can't see Gerhard and Mbato letting us drive back to our cruiser and back to the Lodge after this,' said Roland. 'We have evidence against them. They'll stop at nothing to get it back.'

'So what *do* we do?' asked Ralph.

'Find another way out.' Xai leaned out of the truck window. 'The battery is three-quarters charged. I found explosives too. If we head south-east and break out of Gerhard's reserve we can drive into the Lebombo Mountains. Hide out in the wilderness.'

Niko nodded sadly. 'Fugitives.'

'With the virus spreading like it is, it may be the safest place for now.' Roland gave her a crooked smile. 'Xai and I know the area quite well. We tackled poachers there, years back.'

'Those mountains are a sacred place to my tribe, the San,' Xai said. 'My ancestors settled there over a hundred thousand years ago. There are still San tribes living there today. If we can find them, they will help us. Hide us.'

'But we can't hide for ever,' said Ralph with a shudder, waving everyone towards the truck as the crocodiles slithered closer.

'For ever?' Robyn echoed. 'It's hard enough to imagine getting through the next few hours.'

'Don't give up,' Grant told her softly. 'Thanks to Ralph, we still have that footage you took of Mbato.'

'And we have an eyewitness to what went down in Gauda,' Ralph said, and placed his hand on Niko's shoulder.

'And after all we've seen and learned here,' said Grant, 'with my father's contacts in the Green Freedom Party, we can find a way to smash Mbato's corrupt regime – and bring Gerhard to justice.'

There was a brooding silence, which Niko broke. 'All that's for the future,' she said quietly. 'Right now, let's do all we can to ensure we still have one. Grant, that broken finger of yours needs splinting.'

'There's a first aid kit in what's left of the jeep,' Roland reminded her. 'I'll see what guns and ammo we can salvage here.'

'I'll help,' Ralph said.

'Then I'll get the kit,' said Robyn. She found it, still attached by heavy Velcro to the side of the boot, and picked up a flare gun that had come loose nearby too.

'Help me.'

The woman's voice made her jump. Robyn walked around the wrecked truck and saw Abi lying, shaking and soaked in blood, beside Brad's mangled body.

'That monster crushed my hip.' Abi tried to move, and groaned. 'I can't move. Please . . . if those crocs come for me . . .'

Gripping the flare gun, Robyn walked towards Abi, remembering what the woman had said to her when they'd first met; it seemed like forever ago.

'Look at you, Abi,' Robyn said softly. 'Trying so hard to

act in control when you're so afraid. I can take someone like you . . . and try to help them.' She crouched beside the shivering woman, opened the first aid kit and gave her a morphine shot for the pain. 'Enough lives have been lost today because of who you work for. Don't you think?' She pushed the flare gun into Abi's hand. 'This will help you last till your friends come to pick you up.'

Abi didn't answer. She looked away, her attention turning to the sly crocs lurking on the bank.

As Robyn re-joined the others with the first aid kit in her hand, she saw Grant nod his understanding. She shrugged. 'If you want to change the world,' she said, 'you have to start somewhere. Right?'

'And make what's broken better,' Niko agreed.

Her hand slipped into Robyn's.

Robyn didn't pull away.

His suit torn and bloodied, Gerhard sat in the back of his truck beside Mbato as it raced towards his complex.

'You can't let the Ballantynes get away,' rumbled Mbato, dabbing at the bullet graze on his forearm with a monogrammed handkerchief. 'You stopped me getting the phone back from the boy just so you could play your sick power games. They still have evidence against me. They mustn't be allowed to use it. You've got to stop them.'

'How? I've lost my best people.' Suddenly Gerhard's thin lips puckered in a smile. 'Still. If it comes to it, let them get away.'

'What? You can't lose your nerve now!' spat Mbato. 'The

election's only four months away. You need me in power to hide the fact that your research caused this virus! You need me to push through your plans.'

'And you need me, my funding and my resources to ensure you stay in power.' Gerhard snorted. 'Let the country go into lockdown – what does it matter? Let the whole world.'

'Why?' said Mbato. 'Because that means that everyone will be stuck at home, buying *Predasaur* to play on their consoles, making a mint for you while the rest of the economy collapses?'

'No,' said Gerhard. 'Because people in lockdown are angry people. And we can give the people a target for their anger.' His grin was the merciless grimace of a born predator. 'We can give them Roland Ballantyne . . .'

Xai started up their truck. Ralph laid his head against the soft backrest. Robyn was slumped beside him, her head on Niko's shoulder. *I never imagined I'd get this close to Niko,* she thought. *I never imagined a whole lot of things.*

Grant looked across at her. 'We did it,' he said softly. 'We stayed alive.'

'Luke wasn't so lucky,' Robyn said, and closed her eyes. She thought of Luke, and Ashwin and Indah. *That's why we must keep going*, she told herself. *To make it count for the ones who can't.*

Ralph's body ached, and he longed for sleep. Instead, they'd be driving through a crocodile-infested river, ready to blow their way through a fence. From there, they'd have to head south into threatening mountain territory. Who knew what forces would be ranged against them?

Their ordeal had only just begun.

The truck picked up speed. Ralph closed his eyes. *Get some rest while you can*, he told himself. *You're going to need it.* He thought grimly of poor Luke's last moments . . . of Indah taking herself out of the horror . . . of Ashwin screaming as the crazed beasts had torn at him. Mourning them wasn't enough.

I have to avenge them, Ralph thought. And that meant doing anything necessary to survive. To protect himself and his family. To bend hard times to his will – and triumph, just like his ancestors had.

This is what true Adventurists do, Ralph thought. *Exactly what they must.*

Coming in autumn 2023.

Wilbur Smith is one of the most successful authors in the world, having sold over 130 million copies of his incredible adventure novels. Wilbur died in 2021, leaving behind him a treasure-trove of stories that will delight readers for years to come.

Keith Chapman is a television writer and producer, best known as the creator of children's television programmes *Bob the Builder* and *PAW Patrol*. Keith originates from Norfolk and currently resides in Monaco.

Steve Cole is the best-selling author of over 150 books. His work includes the *Astrosaurs* series, original fiction titles for *Doctor Who*, the *Young Bond* series and *Swarm Rising* co-authored with astronaut Tim Peake. Steve lives and works in Buckinghamshire.

For all the latest information about Wilbur, visit:
www.wilbursmithbooks.com
facebook.com/WilburSmith
www.wilbur-niso-smithfoundation.org

Wilbur Smith donates twenty per cent of profits received from the sale of this copy to The Wilbur & Niso Smith Foundation. The Foundation's focus is to encourage adventure writing and literacy and find new talent.

For more information, please visit
www.wilbur-niso-smithfoundation.org

THE WILBUR & NISO SMITH
FOUNDATION

Thank you for choosing a Hot Key book.

If you want to know more about our authors and what we publish, you can find us online.

You can start at our website

www.hotkeybooks.com

And you can also find us on:

We hope to see you soon!